Nixie the Mermaid

and The Power of Love

AF663320

notionpress.com

Nixie the Mermaid

and The Power of Love

Digangana Suryavanshi

notionpress
.com

Notion Press

Old No. 38, New No. 6

McNichols Road, Chetpet

Chennai - 600 031

Republished by Notion Press 2016

ISBN 978-93-5206-614-8

For the one whom I love more than I love myself, my Nani!

The reason why I stand to be a person like I am today,

For Maa and Papa who made tales after tales

So I be able to sleep well;

I thank and dedicate this to my family

For an incredible upbringing!

Love you all! Thanks!

Contents

Acknowledgement

Writing this novel is very close to me, it's not just writing another fantasy or love story. People have already assumed so much about mermaids that it's very difficult to give it another view! There have been tales and theories trying to prove if they exit or they don't, it's been quite discussed so I had this in my head to give it a different explanation and describe the marine life and mermaids in an altogether different way!

Another reason of putting this up is that I believe that love is really the strongest power on the planet! If you really love someone, your partner, your parents or anybody else, if it's true and pure then there is no better protection to ask for! It protects you and has the power to change anything and everything! Through years and with change in time and people with it, the definition of love has evolved and changed a lot, I firmly wanted to put this at the front that love is not about the give and take, materialistic lifestyle, expectations and their fulfillment.

It can't be judged on this basis, it's about how you truly love each other even if there was nothing around! Life most of the time takes you to a turn where you have to make choices, it puts you to that spot where you truly realize and figure out the kind of person you are and what your beliefs are! It's difficult to find people who really care about you and love you for who you are than what you look like externally! This story is not just about Nixie and William, it's about every single relation humans built for emotional support and how far do they believe in it, it's about the difference in human life and certain emotions that count so much more than what most people think of it.

Relationship have become a part of the social human life, sometimes we miss emotions in them! We quite only read about true love in fairy tales but every individual human experiences are so different from one another that it's no less than a unique tale so if there can be unique stories then fairy tales can also exist, there's no machine that calculates how much you really love but life and its journey is a self-calculator, leave it up to life and you will learn all that you need to know!

I'm humbled to be able to write this novel and I sincerely thank my maternal grandma, my parents and everybody in my family for always standing by me and believing in me. I believe in love and I believe that's beliefs do make a difference. Life is a journey, just try and make it a beautiful one…

For Nixie and William the journey is yet to go on…

Hope you all have a great reading experience! Thank you!

- Digangana Suryavanshi

Chapter 1

The Man Whose Ambition Brought Trouble to the Mermaids!

Everything seemed just like it always was in New York City. The multistoried towers, expensive cars rushing, ambitious people working extremely hard to get where they wish to be. It was a very normal day for everybody except for James. People gave very little time to family and more time to work. It was pretty normal, but there was something strange in this huge commercial building, everybody around was well-dressed and organized, very impressive gesture. But, after a very long time James, the owner of this huge cliff tower seemed to be rushing for something very important and was wrapping his stuff in his cabin, James' cabin seemed to be like the president's cabin as it was so spacious, wide, clean and vibrant, but there right on James' big wide desk, everything was messed up.

James was excited and smiling! It was very strange because James never rushed for anything even if it was a life-changing meeting. Something was wrong that evening because James being so rich and busy rarely wrapped up his stuff on his own. But he did do that six months ago. We get that from past experience. It looked like James had forgotten to shave and dye his hair and his age was very obvious from his gray hair and graying beard. But that wasn't something to worry about because he was already forty-five.

James wasn't the right person to blame on his looks, being unmarried and devoted to work, by that he looked great! He had a strong personality and fire in his eyes. He was not much like a muscular man but was very slim and fit. His desperate and curious constantly moving eyes suddenly set on a book. He looked more relaxed than before. Immediately after, he looked at the book as his forehead crinkle relaxed a bit and he also smiled looking at the book and promptly kept the book in his handbag. The book seemed to be very special to James.

It looked quite old but was well preserved and wrapped in a beautiful looking case. The book was titled with a name and had a sketch on its cover. It was barely possible to look at it as James promptly kept it in. Henry walked in with a briefcase in his right hand. Henry was well-dressed and little younger than James He had fewer wrinkles and no gray hair. He was clean shaven and right above his suit pocket, there was a badge that mentioned his post as a manager. James didn't wear such a badge. As Henry walked in, without wasting time, he said, with respect for James, "Sir, your private jet is all set to leave!"

James looked intensely at Henry. He smiled with most awaiting attitude. He looked forward for something very important and special. He just nodded. Meanwhile, two of his bodyguards walked in with an identity card around their neck, mentioning their posts as bodyguards. They had a tanned skin tone and poker faces. They were respectful towards James and James looked at all of them waiting for him. There was clear understanding between them! He picked his leather handbag that wasn't too heavy and said, "Let's go!"

Speaking only about the important things pretty much described that James was not much fond of talking a lot but never lost his charm.

Henry and James' bodyguards made way for James to walk out first. They followed him to the lift. James walked like he was royalty with tremendous dignity. Each step he took bought a smile to his face. James walked into the elevator and Henry and his bodyguards followed him. One of the bodyguards pressed the button to the lobby on the ground floor. The elevator landed on the ground floor. James walked out first and the rest followed him.

Everybody in the lobby greeted James and politely said 'good evening sir.' James nodded and went his way. The staff members who were just walking around made distance with him out of respect and intending to not cross his way, they gracefully greeted him and those who were seated stood up, showing respect.

James reached the entrance. Right outside the door, there were five white cars and James' team waiting for him.

James' set up team included Max, Lisa, Kevin, Rebecca, Leo, Drake and Charles and Max was the head of the team. Max looked fresh and enthusiastic as always. He wore a big cowboy hat as it was his trademark outfit. He also wore his weird belt and shoe that he used regularly. He had a minor beard that mostly had white hair and so did his hands and legs, they were seen as he wore cargo shots and a mid-sleeved shirt on top of a t-shirt.

Max's team consisted of young adults and very sharp-minded people. They were extremely casually dressed with a great working attitude and did not believe in wasting time.

Understanding and cooperation was valuable and their strength, they were also witty and nasty to one another for fun sake sometimes. They wore identity cards with their names and positions except for Max, as he was the team leader so he took certain things for granted but it was not much to worry about. He knew his work well.

Max initiated the conversation and spoke out of respect and extended his hand to James and greeted him simultaneously. "Good to see you again, Sir!" In response, James smiled but his smile was as intrigue as his body language and formally hugged him.

Max said, "Now we're all addicted to travel with you and setting up things for you once every six months! It's commendable how you are so precise sir?"

James looked around and thought something that made him look extremely desperate, and then replied, "Yes, of course! I am used to travelling with all of you. After this rushed lifestyle that I lead, I need some time to myself, so it's a good way out!"

It seemed as if James was hiding something important and just filling people's brain by saying something that wasn't the real reason why he travelled to the islands that were at a long distance, once every six months. But nobody ever dared to ask him the real reason - not even his mother, who already was aware of his only ambition in life but she wasn't sure what he really wanted. James' ambition was still a mystery to everybody except for his mom who knew his ambition but just considered it a dream. His dad wasn't doing well in terms of health and barely remembered anything or anyone. Different people had their different set of doubts and James knew most of them but never bothered any of it. His mom only knew the half story and rest was in dilemma for her just like everybody else.

Taking some time, James casually said, “Let’s leave!”

Everyone sat up alert and Max said, “Sure!”

Everybody waited till James got into the car. Before he did, he softly asked, looking at Henry, “Luggage and all?”

Henry replied, “All set Sir!”

The strange part was that James was not used to asking about luggage. All this was a matter of routine for the staff. This pretty much described his desperation. James was reserved, but was still excited and said, pressing his lips like kids do out of excitement, “Okay then!” He sat in the car that was right in the middle. All the cars were expensive and clean enough to grab anyone’s attention. They were milky white with added shades of sliver to it, on the curves, and also had luxurious seating arrangements inside. After James sat in, his manager sat right next to him. The driver shut the door without a noise. It was very gently and precisely done.

Meanwhile, the set up team sat in the car right behind James’ car. His security staff sat in the car ahead of James’ car while the first and the last car came in with the luggage, the security and his bodyguards. James relaxed in the car. His expressions were obvious that he was extremely happy and energetic. It looked like James was finally being the real him. The cars smoothly geared up and left when the street lights turned on.

In just some time at night, when the roads were brightened with lights and looked even more beautiful, they reached the airport. Right after the security check James and his set up team headed to the private jet and settled in quickly. Sometime later, when James looked up at the sky, the jet took off.

James sat by the window and looked outside. He seemed relaxed. He pulled his tie down and undid the top button of his shirt and took off his blazer. He closed his eyes for a few seconds and relaxed, looking out of the window. He could see nothing else except for the dark and gray clouds.

Next day at dawn, when James wasn't asleep, his team was. When the white clouds were visible and the atmosphere seemed clear. The pilot announced the time left for landing. James was awake and peacefully listening to the announcement. James got off the bed and glanced outside the window. He wasn't able to see much. He smiled, thinking that he was close to his destination. James refreshed himself and changed his clothes.

In just a few minutes, the jet landed in Finland. James was excited. So was his team. As soon as the door opened, wasting no time, James walked out. He looked casual, dressed in shorts and a loose t-shirt, and comfortable, light shoes. He carried his handbag along. He seemed very protective of it. He looked everywhere and tried to gaze at the place. But he didn't know what he was looking for. He smiled for no reason and looked back at his team and moved down the staircase. His team followed.

After the Finland staff checked and confirmed their presence in Finland, they proceeded to the helicopters that waited for them. James and his manager reserved a helicopter and the other was occupied by the rest of the team and all the luggage. Soon, the helicopters departed and James was busy reading his dairy. It was difficult to figure out what the book was called as James kept the book on his lap and was reading silently.

It was then when Henry said, after observing James for quite some time, "Sir, I'm a bit curious. May I ask you something?"

James glanced at Henry and replied, "Ya, sure!" The way he said it was very relaxed. Henry said, "Sir, why do wish to visit such a dangerous island? High tides hit the island every now and then and sometimes even the island sinks in!"

James straightened his shoulder and became alert. The question seemed important to him. After thinking for a while, he sarcastically smiled as if he knew that he was lying, but said, "Well, actually, I want to find out more about the island and also that I like danger. No worries, we've already known the weather forecast well, things will be fine!"

Henry was confused and worried about James. He said, "Sir, I did find something about that island. But it sounds like a rumor. People say there is magic on that island!"

James' gesture turned alert. It was like he was interested and said, "I still like danger! All for the good!" This was an indirect message to Henry that he would visit the island. James and Henry had been working together for a really long time. As far as Henry knew James, he had realized that James wasn't interested in the talk and this was the reason why Henry dissuaded the topic by agreeing.

James was thinking about the island and peeped outside murmuring, "Magic, interesting!" He looked way more curious and desperate than before.

After some time, when the sun shone brightly, they had reached the island. The place looked like heaven in the middle of the ocean. It was far away from all dirt. It was extremely clean with crystal clear water that was literally glittering.

The color green spread around the place. Butterflies were flying around like they were dancing and playing with the wind and different species of plants and flowers. It looked like a magical world. The island looked untouched. The moment the helicopters landed, James walked out with his handbag and his team followed him.

James was unable to believe what he saw. It was extremely beautiful! James looked around and so did everyone else. They were pleasantly surprised. James slowly walked to the shore and touched the waves. He removed his shoes and socks and stood there, as he took a deep breath with tremendous passion that was obvious by his body language and facial expressions!

Max was right behind James. They were focusing on fixing requirements and attending to requirements for James. They were peaceful enough. There were all possible luxurious set for James and everything as per his convenience. Max said loudly, "Everybody! Let's get to work, we need to get it done soon!" He was extremely loud. James just did not bother turning around to see what they were doing. He was lost in his own world and nobody could interrupt him.

Time passed by. It was dark everywhere. There was too much moisture in the air but it was still cold and calm. James lay on the beach, holding a cup of coffee. His book was right beside him. James looked at the stars in the sky. They looked beautiful, like never before. Stars are lost in cities, but on the island, it seemed like they ruled. They seemed like diamonds. James had tears in his eyes. It definitely wasn't just that he found them beautiful, but something beyond beauty. He could connect with them. He definitely had some relation with them that wasn't clear by then!

Suddenly Henry came by and disturbed James thought process, saying, "Sir, may I show you around the tent?"

Since James was lost, it took a few seconds for him to be fine but then he was quite settled. While standing up with his book in hand and a cup of coffee in another, he said, "Yeah sure!"

They turned around and walked into the tent. His team was busy wrapping their stuff up so they could leave at the earliest.

A big tent that included all requirements and luxuries like packed food, water arrangement, communication systems, a boat, safety bag, tubes, first aid and a lot more were placed. It seemed like the set up team also cared about the looks of the tent as it looked beautiful but smart.

Henry said, with respect, "Sir, everything is all set -"

He was supposed to continue but then James interrupted saying, "I know all that! Where's my guitar?" This proved that his guitar meant more than anything else to him.

Henry smiled and pointed at the guitar saying, "We know how important that is to you, just can't miss that!"

James smiled and said, "Ya right! Let's meet after three days. You can leave now. Apparently mom will accompany you to pick me up as she said. Ask her about her plans before you leave from New York, okay?"

Henry agreed saying, "Sure Sir! See you soon! Take care. Sir, just in case of an emergency, we're leaving a helicopter for you. You can fly, too!" James dramatically nodded and said, "Ya, ya… I know!"

Henry smiled and left. They came out of the tent and immediately after the helicopter left and everyone waved their hands. James looked at the waves curiously thinking about something very important to him. James held the book tight and brought it near his chest. He was very affectionate towards the book. He sat down on the beach. James had tears in his eyes and he looked up at the sky and began speaking, looking at the stars in particular. "Grandpa, I really miss you!"

James said, "I remember my struggle that I had to do to take this dairy from you because I was too young!" he said. This refreshed his memories. James said, "I remember you explained how important this dairy is to our family. I know our ancestors wrote this dairy when they saw a mermaid! This dairy has everything about them, I know it is precious!"

Finally!

It was then when James mentioned what the dairy was about.

He said, when a teardrop rolled down his cheek, "I know that this dairy is our family's honor and it has been passed to the new generation. Everybody else just kept it for the sake of it, but grandpa, this book is my ambition, I was ten when you passed away and this is the thing you left for me. Grandpa, for your sake, I really wish to see a mermaid!"

This one-sided conversation described everything by itself. It was a complete story right from where it started.

James said, "I know that our ancestors lost their eyes because of the power of the mermaids. I know that mermaids are pure and all humans aren't that pure. Our ancestors worshiped the King of the Ocean so they did not lose their life. Otherwise, they would have. But you know, grandpa, they wrote this dairy when they were blind. You know how much

I love you! For you and for them, I want to see a mermaid, I won't regret my death, please grandpa, help me live my ambition!"

So this was James' ambition! He wanted to be able to see a real mermaid once! How interesting was that? James said, wiping his tears, "Grandpa, I want to see and feel that golden ocean when a lot of mermaids travel and ignite light! How beautiful and peaceful that would be! Please help me, please!"

James was an extremely ambitious man. All his abnormal behavior proved to be very convincing. James seemed emotional. As he closed his eyes, in just a fraction of a second, something happened. As James mentioned and the dairy described it, a lot of mermaids travelled underwater and a glowing light was seen on the surface of the water. It was golden and the most beautiful ocean light that anybody could ever see. As James opened his eyes, he realized that something had happened. But, a sound came out of his tent and it distracted him. He curiously ran inside.

He seemed to be a little scared. When he went into the tent, he noticed that it was nothing but air pressure that moved the curtain's rope which was knotted in the middle of the curtain. The hanging metal weight banged against the guitar strings. That was why the strings seemed to be making a sound. Something snapped James and he again ran to the shore. The air pressure had risen. Tall trees literally bent down and a very pleasant sound of waves was audible. It wasn't there before. All these sudden changes made James realize that maybe before he left for the tent, he did see the golden ocean, exactly like it was mentioned in the dairy!

James was stunned. He was extremely happy and surprised. He immediately looked at the stars and said, "Magic! I'm sure

I'll be able to reach my ambition here, I can find the mermaids! Thanks, grandpa!"

James suddenly looked confident and fearless. He was ready for any sort of situation. It was a really long night for James as he was extremely restless. He just couldn't be patient anymore.

The next bright morning brought hope to James. He woke up with the sunrise. It wasn't a mystery anymore, what the dairy was about and what was so special in it. James stood on the shore of the island and the waves touched his feet. His shoe was somewhere at the back. James was casually dressed and prayed. He was saying something that wasn't audible at all. His passion and curiosity to see a mermaid was clear and obvious on his face. He closed eyes and at the same time, something very fast and furious happened under water. It ignited too much light. The island brightened and birds started singing. Butterflies seemed dancing and trees were waving in the breeze. Nature celebrated, as if it was some very important and auspicious occasion.

James opened his eyes and noticed the golden ocean. He couldn't believe that he was living his ambition and something could be this beautiful! James was surprised and uttered "Beautiful! Thank you God! Thank you grandpa!"

In the depths of the ocean, a lot of mermaids travelled. They ignited their golden light. It was so bright that hardly anything was seen except for their glittery tails which moved like the tails of fish. It looked extremely slippery and smooth. After focusing on how they looked, their hair was noticeable. They were light bright blue in color and really long and flawless. They travelled at an extremely high speed and the light brightened everything around them just like a tube light, except it was brighter and more magical. They were really furious.

Upon the island, James hoped to see a mermaid. He was excited and curious. He couldn't believe that he was so close to his dream, every moment was like a year!

James whispered, looking up at the sky, "Grandpa, I wish to see a mermaid! Please help me, please!" He walked back into the tent.

The moment James' passionately wished to see a mermaid, and since his passion had no self-centered meaning or purpose, two of the mermaids stopped underwater and as they did, it seemed like the world stopped for a few seconds. Right after the peace of a few seconds, they held their heads high and furiously moved upwards, as if they were cutting the water.

They swam in the opposite direction to the weight of the water, extremely fast and furious. Their aura was very graceful. It was incredible essence that any living being could ever have. They moved furiously, turning and twisting like they were playing and dancing. They looked like they were having fun, and were energetic and happy! Suddenly, both of them stopped. Strong waves hit the shore!

As they stopped, James played the guitar. Somehow, he was getting distracted every now and then by just the thought of mermaids. He stopped playing as he saw something and kept the guitar aside. He walked forward, but then thought, maybe it was an illusion. He got back to playing the guitar and said, "Grandpa as you said, mermaids like music! I hope to see them soon!" Playing the guitar and worshipping the Ocean King honestly did work for him.

Both mermaids were gradually coming to the surface of the water. They were far away from where James was. Soon, a big rock magically appeared on the surface of the water which was far away and James paid no attention to it as he thought it was there already. But, the rock was created by both the mermaids and had just come up. They took the support of the rock to hide behind it and to be able to see James, whereas he wasn't able to see the mermaids.

They kept their hands on the rock. They looked like human hands covered by thin and transparent, glittery gelatin paper that webbed their fingers which also had enough of a distance so that they could use their palms just like humans do. They appeared like a combination of human and amphibian hands. They had slippery skin and water didn't stay on it at all. They had golden nails, no nail paint but real natural beauty that glittered more than nail paint would. They gradually came out of the water and their faces were seen. They were gorgeous! Beauty with no stain at all! They looked very different from humans, although their upper half was like a human body. The lower half was like a fish. They had light blue hair. They had light blue and deep eyes that looked spiritual. Their eyelashes were light blue, and were long and properly curved. They also had light blue eyebrows, very delicate red-pink lips and natural pink blush on their checks and on their noses.

They had long and beautiful necks, and were extremely graceful. It seemed like they wore pearl outfits on the upper half but it wasn't any outfit - they had it since birth. It seemed as if they had worn earrings but even that was natural, since it glittered, it seemed to be like jewelry but it wasn't, they had a really strong fragrance that spread around. Nature was celebrating their presence. Little flowers immediately bloomed.

Butterflies emerged and birds were singing. Trees waved as if they were saying hello! It all looked pleasant and calm!

James was playing his guitar and the mermaids enjoyed music. James suddenly stopped playing because he was getting distracted by just the thought of mermaids. He could feel their presence but unfortunately couldn't see them! Both mermaids looked at each other and smiled. The younger mermaid looked like an eighteen year old and the older mermaid looked about twenty-five. The younger mermaid was extremely excited looking at a human, whereas the older mermaid was too interested and curious. Her excitement wasn't that obvious as the younger mermaid. They read James' brain and learned everything about humans in just a few seconds through magic. The younger mermaid started the conversation and said, "Very good language! I don't believe humans have to speak so they can convey their thoughts! We just have to think and our thoughts are said, how different is that?"

Nothing beats the innocence on the younger mermaid's face!

The older mermaid smiled and teased but gracefully said, "Then why are you talking?"

The younger mermaid understood that older mermaid was teasing her and said "Hmmm! Because it has a different sort of fun in it! Don't you think so?"

This was a casual friendly conversation. The older mermaid said, "Yes, you're right!" Both laughed. Their laughter sounded like pleasant waves. James noticed this sudden change in sound and exclaimed in a low voice, "Such a pleasant sound! I know what this is!"

James realized that he had read about it in the dairy and was able to feel the mermaid's presence and it made him extremely happy! The older mermaid said. "I wish to hear more music from him!" Suddenly, something stroked James and he began playing the guitar again. The mermaid did that. But James was so frustrated that he stopped playing and said, "Aaaah! I want to see a Mermaid!" Since both mermaids wished to hear more music and James stopped, they got a bit disturbed. But they were not disturbed like humans get. They were still graceful.

The younger mermaid said, "Why did he stop playing? I liked it!"

The older mermaid said, "He's got a tremendous passion to see us!" The younger mermaid and older mermaid were on different tracks. The younger mermaid said, "Hmmm, true. Humans have so much to do!"

The older mermaid was still on her different track and said, "Should I ask him to play more?"

The younger mermaid exclaimed out of excitement, "No! You can force him to play music right from here, why do you have to go there?"

The older mermaid insisted and said, "I know, I can but I want to sing with him!"

The younger mermaid asked, "Why do wish to invite danger and what if he asks something?"

The older mermaid showed magic in her finger tips and smiled and said, "He won't be able to ask!"

The younger was a little convinced and said, "Okay! Take care!"

The older mermaid laughed saying, “I’m not going for a war!”

The younger mermaid was worried but very casually said, “Meeting and greeting any human is no less than waging a war!”

Both loudly laughed. Gradually, the older mermaid headed towards the island while the younger mermaid was still behind the rock, watching the happenings. Through magic James was distracted, he was feeling weird but wasn’t able to look at the ocean!

Soon, the older mermaid came on the shore of the island, on the other end that James couldn’t see. As she came out of the water, she turned into a gorgeous young woman. She looked beautiful and was dressed just like a normal woman. She wore blue denim jeans and a casual top, just like anybody else would ware on an island. She left her long hair loose.

She had no makeup but was still beautiful. Her clothes were wet when she stepped out of the water and that was why she closed her eyes for a few seconds. As she opened her eyes and looked down at what she was wearing, it was all dry! She then looked at the younger mermaid. Both smiled. James had no idea what was going on. The older mermaid walked towards James who was reading his dairy. He thought somebody was behind him. He turned around out of fear. A young woman stood before him. James was stunned and immediately got up.

Before James could ask her anything, the older mermaid introduced herself saying, “Hi, my name is Yara, you play good music! It caught my attention. Please play more and I’ll sing along!”

James was shocked at how a woman suddenly appeared right in front of him. He wanted to ask and know more about her but he just couldn't. He was trying to speak but he was completely absentminded and mute because of older mermaid's magic. Yara's magical powers didn't allow James to question her presence Then, he finally decided to not question her but to simply compliment her and this is why he could finally talk, he said, "You are beautiful, very beautiful, I mean extremely beautiful!"

Yara casually smiled, looking at James and pointed at the guitar. James smiled back and picked up his guitar. James played music and Yara sang just the notes, not the lyrics. The younger mermaid was happy looking at Yara and was dancing and playing with the water.

After Yara and James played music, it was time for Yara to leave. She looked at James and told him, "Thank you so much. I have to go now, nice to meet you!" saying this, Yara turned and left.

James didn't want her to leave. He felt some sort of affection towards her and she looked stunning. James was disturbed. His gaze turned impure for a few seconds towards Yara. Then, he stopped Yara. He grabbed her hand tight and bought her close to himself. Yara was shocked. Before she could use her magical powers, she got extremely restless and fell on the ground. In the meantime, the younger mermaid was tremendously stressed.

She tried using magic, but it didn't work. She found herself feeling helpless. When she realized that she couldn't use magic, she burst into tears. Her teardrops turned into pearls as they rolled down her check and fell in the water. Yara tried to reach the water but failed. She was sweating and restless. James couldn't understand what was happening. Just then, Yara became unconscious and she appeared in her original form as a mermaid.

Suddenly, Yara ignited and a bright light burst through her form. It threw James away by quite a distance. James fell on the sand. He was sweating and it looked like he was dying of heat and that his body couldn't take it. He knew by then that he was going to die but he was happy as he had finally achieved his ambition. He looked up at the sky and said, "Thank you!" He could barely speak clearly. He gradually turned into ashes. Nothing was left of him. Yara was unconscious and lost her light. The younger mermaid was extremely shocked and her head started spinning. She controlled herself and reached the island. In no time, she lifted Yara and went underwater. The clouds turned gray and the atmosphere seemed like a funeral. Even the birds cried and trees were still. James' ambition had brought trouble to both mermaids!

Chapter 2

The Battle for Love Tears Begins

The younger mermaid had reached underwater and then she suddenly stopped and looked around. There were some really annoying creatures and they seemed to dislike the light ignited from the mermaid. They were dull and dark. Their eyes were bright enough and they were disgustingly looking at the younger mermaid and Yara without blinking. Their upper half was like that of a human and lower half was like that of a fish.

They were just like mermaids, but they had stinking red hair and big owl-like eyes, dirty nails and sharp teeth like sharks and little black spots on their body. They were brown from top to bottom and looked dangerous. The younger mermaid was fearless. Her expression pretty much described that it was a routine for her, she grunted, looking at them without any prominent attention to anyone of them in particular. They were called the water-girls.

The younger mermaid looked down where it seemed like that the depths were going to the end. The younger mermaid knew what she was supposed to do. She used magic and all the water-girls left as a beam of golden light put the darkness to an end. It looked like a magical world had just begun where the younger mermaid moved on from the place where the water-girls lived. The place seemed like it was, before her presence. It consisted of blue light and all the water-girls appeared again.

This process seemed like an opening and closing of an unseen door in the middle of the ocean. The younger mermaid had finally reached the beautiful water world where she lived. She stood still like a statue with moist eyes and was looking at somebody.

The place looked like heaven. It was bright with golden light and some butterfly-like water creatures glided around in several colors. Different species of light plants were seen. The place had expensive gems, silver and gold scattered around with no importance being attached to them. The younger mermaid moved ahead to a big beautiful baby pink flower with extremely delicate petals. The flower was almost six feet in width and three feet in height. It was the most beautiful flower anybody could have ever seen. The younger mermaid placed unconscious Yara on that flower gently. She lost control over her emotions after that and burst into tears. She was torn apart and cried bitterly. All her tears turned into beautiful pearls. She turned around and all other mermaids came closer. There were hundreds of them, about five came closer to the younger mermaid as they seemed close and important to her. For mermaids, thoughts and feelings were not conveyed in word - they just had to think and their thoughts were passed on from one to the other. One of them consoled the younger mermaid and said, "Everything will be fine!"

All the mermaids were in tears and already knew what had happened. The younger mermaid said, "This was all my fault! I shouldn't have let Sakhi go near a human!"

"Sakhi" was the common word that they used to address each other. They never referred to each other by name.

Another mermaid consoled her, patting her shoulder. "No, it's not your fault! It's nobody's fault!" Another mermaid added, "Yes, this was meant to be and maybe it was fate!"

The younger mermaid was crying bitterly. "She is more than a friend to me, I have to get back her to life!"

Another mermaid said, "But we don't have that much power to fix all this and we don't even know why this happened!"

The younger mermaid looked at them and said, "There must be a way out, I can't let it go like this!"

Then she suddenly realized that she could ask the Ocean King and said, "We can ask help from the King! He surely can sort this out and get Sakhi back to life!"

The younger mermaid had some hope and all the mermaids exchanged looks. They thought she was right and that they must ask the King for help. Soon, they formed a big circle, closed their eyes, joined hands, bowed their heads and began praying. Soon, a big bright golden ball appeared right in the middle of the circle. The mermaids scattered and stood in rows right behind the big round bright golden ball. The ball started turning into a figure that was extremely bright like the sun. In a few seconds, it had turned into a human figure on the upper half and the lower half just consisted of water. It seemed like water was connected to him. It was a male human figure that looked tremendously calm and graceful he had a very strong personality with extremely calm eyes and expression. It had dark blue eyes, blue and silver eye lashes, eye brows and a long beard.

A beautiful crown made of gold, pearls and precious gems sat on his head. It was impossible to guess his age. He lived from the time the earth was created but looked like he was no older than seventy. His power was clearly visible on his face. The King already knew what had happened. He was aware of the past, present and future. But he was calm and confident, with an all-knowing smile. He looked serious but not stressed. As he appeared, the mermaids bowed their heads for his presence and were respectable towards him. The younger mermaid was embarrassed and was struggling to face the King but she was honest and willingly wanted to confess the truth and was also desperate to find the solution and fix everything right just for her friend.

Meanwhile on the island, two helicopters landed. It was time to pick up James, as he said. James' mom Rita walked out of the helicopter and his team followed. James' mom was a tall and aged lady. She was slim and well-maintained. She dressed gracefully with matching shades and shoes. She ran happily towards the tent and looking inside the tent, she was shocked and had an expressionless face out of shock. She then turned around to Henry and James' set up team and asked, "Where is James? He isn't in here and the tent is filled with water!"

Henry was shocked and asked, "Is Sir not in there?"

Rita was panicking and said, "No!"

Henry and James then came running to the tent. They were all shocked, looking at everything that was messed up. James' guitar was broken. Nobody could figure out what had happened on the island. They scattered around and yelled out James' name with the hope that they would be able to find him. But it failed and they could not find him. James' mom was stranded and had tears in her eyes. She tried to control herself and hide her emotions so that nobody could see her.

Somewhere, she had a strong feeling that James was dead and that they would never be able to see him again. Soon, James' manager called up the investigation team to find out where James was and in what condition he was in.

Henry said, with complete authority and orderliness, "I want you and your team here on the island as soon as possible. Address details are available with Ron. Come with tour equipment. Someone's lost here!" Henry hung up. He did not mention that James was lost because he knew that if he'd mention that, the media and staff would pull out different stories.

He wanted to avoid that. He didn't want to let anyone panic unnecessarily because he believed that James was fine, or at least that he was trying his best to avoid negative thoughts. He was scared that they might have to hear extremely bad and sad news! Henry looked at Rita and both had tears in eyes. Underwater, the younger mermaid could barely utter a word. She was so embarrassed and awkward. Reducing her awkwardness, the King said, "I am aware of everything that has happened!"

The younger mermaid looked at the King with hopeful eyes and said, "I am ready to do anything. Please get Sakhi back to life!"

The King said with a serious expression on his face, "It's not that easy, little mermaid! It is not as easy as you think it is!"

The younger mermaid understood that if the King was saying it was difficult, it must be difficult. She then said "King! There must be a way! Please tell me!" The King said, "There is one!"

The younger mermaid said, "What is it?"

The King knew that it was difficult but looking at the younger mermaid's determination he said, "Love tears!" Nobody around knew what he was talking about. They looked at him curiously. The King said, "If a man falls in love with a mermaid, remember it must be true love, not lust, and later when the mermaid would break his heart, the tears the man would shed must be collected and sprinkled on your Sakhi. It is only then that she will be granted another life!"

The younger mermaid was blank for a moment. Another mermaid said, out of curiosity and concern, "But King if a human falls in love with a mermaid, the mermaid will be in love too!"

Another mermaid said, "Yes, love can't be one-sided!"

The King said, "It doesn't matter if the mermaid is in love or not. It must be true love from the human's side! That is why it's a test of the power of love towards your Sakhi!"

Another mermaid said, "But why is the solution like this?" The younger mermaid just couldn't understand any of this. The King said, "This is because a human touched the purest living being on earth with an impure and dirty gaze. That has led to this situation. Only a human's true love can fix this!"

The younger mermaid said with determination, "King! My love for Sakhi is beyond this test. If this is the only way out, I accept it!" The King and all the mermaids could see clear passion in the younger mermaid's eyes. Every other mermaid was shocked as they knew it wasn't an easy task. They were all in tears. The King said, "It's not easy! It is very challenging!"

The younger mermaid nodded, accepting whatever it was. The King put the conditions forward. "After you turn into a human, you will be completely like them and behave like them. You will think and speak like them. You won't be able to give thoughts to anybody so they move according to you and will not even be able to read anybody's thoughts. You will be able to know anybody's past but not their future. You won't be able to use magic and figure out the truth and falsehood with magic. You will only be able to use magic for self defense and regular life requirements. The most important thing is that you won't be able to turn back into a mermaid until you find your true lover and take his love tears. You have to find true love from the place that men belonged because of whom your Sakhi is suffering! Also you will age as a human being and if you don't be able to find love tears and die as human then your soul won't rest in peace!"

Listening to all this, every mermaid was stunned. Without wasting any more time, the younger mermaid promptly said, "I accept it; I just want Sakhi to be fine, that's all I wish for!"

The King smiled. The younger mermaid said, "But won't this be like cheating somebody?"

The King said, smiling, "Every individual on earth works one way or the other and their work results in what they deserve. Don't worry. You and that human will get justice. Every task isn't right or wrong. This is the only way to grant your Sakhi another life. You will now have to decide if this is right or wrong or if you want to do it or not!"

The younger mermaid said, "I accept with no doubt!"

The King said, "Tomorrow before sunrise, you will enter the human world!"

The younger mermaid thanked the King. That's all she was able to say! She knew that the task wasn't easy and maybe she would be heartbroken later but she was really determined on what she was going to do. Sakhi meant more to her than her own life did. The younger mermaid had no idea what was going to come next. She definitely knew that she had to do this. The King then disappeared!

Three helicopters landed on the island. A huge investigation team walked out. A group of twelve middle-aged men with a bunch of technical devices walked out. Rita, Henry and Max's team was highly stressed. They sat down on the sand. Everybody got up when they saw the investigation team. Rita wasn't in a position to say anything. That was why Henry came forth and said, "I want you to find out where Sir is!" The team's head, Josh said, "Sir!"

Henry clarified, specifying himself and getting more emotional, "Mr. James Black was on the island for the past three days. But now, he isn't here and we have no idea where and how he is, find him!" The investigation team was shocked but maintained professionalism and said, "Sure we will, don't worry!"

Henry escaped. He couldn't control his emotions anymore. The investigation team started their work. Rita noticed some melted gold and a diamond with it on the sand. It was partially covered with sand. She took it out after some effort and hid it under her handkerchief. She gradually opened and brought it close to her. She burst into tears but did not make a sound.

She understood what must have happened. She was so stressed that her nerves were visible. It looked nerve-wracking! She was breaking from within and all she murmured was, "He finally reached his dream, my son!" She wiped her tears and sat in shock with a poker face. She was red out of stress and pain! The investigation team found a shoe in the water. It was hung between two rocks. After some struggle, they pulled it out. After some discussion among themselves, they reached a conclusion. Josh came to Henry and said sadly, "I am so sorry to say this, but we think Sir is no more!"

Henry literally collapsed and said, "What?"

Josh had tears in her eyes and continued seriously. "The investigation proved that Sir had slept on the shore last night and did not realize anything due to his sound sleep and due to high tide, he died!"

Henry was shocked and aggressively said, "How can you prove that?"

Josh said, "We can't prove it but he isn't alive. We're sorry!" Everything and everyone was silent. They just couldn't think of anything! Henry walked towards Rita and the investigation team. He said, crying while he was speaking, but still trying to maintain respect and dignity for Rita, "Madam we are sorry, Sir is no more!"

Rita already knew it. She could barely react to it and the rest of them understood it as a position of shock! Rita's tears were falling down but there was no expression. She looked messed up and said, "Please leave me alone for some time. Then we will leave. I don't want anybody to touch anything now. Wrap this later. Not now. We will just leave, I want you all to sit in the helicopters and take off."

Henry was shattered too and said, "But madam we don't' have a proof yet, investigation maybe false!"

Rita interrupted and said, "It's an order, go!"

They left immediately in the helicopters. After settling, they waited for Rita to come. Rita walked towards the dairy that was on the ground. She picked it up and exclaimed, "It's all because of you. I don't want you!" She threw the dairy in the island and looked at it with disgust; she just couldn't bare her son's death! Rita knew everything that was going on in James' life, but she found herself feeling helpless. She couldn't stop him from doing so.

She knew that James was extremely passionate to see a mermaid. One way or the other, this was going to happen. She felt broken because she could have stopped all this, but didn't. She had some really mixed emotions. At that moment, she couldn't even tell anybody what had happened. She needed really strong support! But then walked into the helicopter and they all left! The island looked like a place of funeral!

Underwater, the younger mermaid was shaken but still had the confidence to fix everything. The other mermaids came close. One of them tapped her on her shoulder. She was trying to be normal, but couldn't help it. The younger mermaid wanted to do all this because she had real love for her Sakhi! One of the mermaids among them said, "What you wish to do isn't possible!"

The younger mermaid knew that the task was tough and said, "Why not, it is possible and it will happen!"

All the mermaids wanted to convince the younger mermaid not to take this step. They also wanted to tell her that this could turn her life upside down. She may also have to regret this for the rest of her life. Another mermaid said, "You don't understand. We know that you love her a lot. But if a human falls in love with you, even you will be in love! It's going to be impossible to live like a mermaid anymore!"

The younger mermaid was aware of everything. She still wanted to take a chance and do it for Sakhi's sake. She said with determination and confidence, "I know! But I am prepared to face anything, because I want Sakhi to be fine. Maybe it's a test to check on my power of love for Sakhi. I will willingly give and pass the test!" The younger mermaid then began to cry bitterly and sat down, taking the support of a big flower. She was broken on the inside, but also aware that she was at a point where she just couldn't be weak at all. All the mermaids supported her with the attitude that they might not be completely convinced with what she was doing and the kind of decision she took but told her that they would always stand by her, wherever she needed them! Then the next morning, before sunrise, all the mermaids gathered and prayed. The King appeared and looked at the younger mermaid. "Are you ready for this? You can still change your decision!"

The younger mermaid had no tears but just determination in her eyes. "No turning back now, I'm ready!"

The King then said, "I will give you protection so if you come under any human contact that isn't pure, even then, you won't turn back into a mermaid!"

The younger mermaid nodded and the King closed his eyes. He lifted his hand up, twisted his fingers downward and accumulated energy in his hand. He let go of the accumulated energy into the younger mermaid and right from the tail till her face, the energy moved and lifted her high. The younger mermaid glowed like nobody else did. Then, the energy sat with her for her protection. The King smiled and looked at the younger mermaid and said, "Time to leave!" The younger mermaid was stuck in her own thought. She was nervous. "Sure!" They looked at each other with the hope that she would pass the test of the power of love for Sakhi!

Chapter 3

In Search of True Love in Another World

The Ocean King then moved and a few mermaids including the younger one, followed him. The rest stood with Yara to take care of her. They reached the surface. When they travelled, all that was possible to see, was too much light. After they reached the surface, they stopped and looked at each other. The younger mermaid already knew what she was supposed to do. She looked at the King and the other mermaids. They had tears in their eyes. Everybody was emotional although the younger mermaid was trying to be emotionally strong and fighting her tears. The King looked at the younger mermaid seriously, "You have been here for a long time. This place might not allow you to leave so fast. You know that each world has two faces - a positive and a negative face! Do not turn back now, just go on, good luck!"

The younger mermaid understood and bowed her head. She shared glances with the rest of the mermaids and moved ahead. The King and the other mermaids left for home, underwater.

Whatever the King said proved to be right. When the younger mermaid moved on, her speed decreased as if the water force wasn't allowing her to move. But fighting it, with all her energy, she carried on but when the force didn't work to stop her, she started hearing a lot of sounds that included her and Yara 's voices, laughing, giggling, voices and the sound of Yara saying, "Promise me that you won't ever leave me alone!"

Younger mermaid said, "I promise!"

The younger mermaid stopped for a few seconds but remembered what the King said, "Do not turn back!" Everything was fine - but suddenly, it started getting dark like something was trying to stop her. A few pairs of big, round, red eyes were visible. The younger mermaid willingly decided not to pay attention to anything. She got her speed back and moved on smoothly without further complications.

As soon as the younger mermaid reached the surface of the water, strong waves hit the beach. The waves looked golden. Nobody was on the beach at that time and trees swung in the breeze. Birds began twittering and the sky was orange. It was drizzling a little and the sun was about to rise. The sun's rays were clearly visible and along with the sunrise, the younger mermaid walked out of the water. As she came out, she transformed into a human. It looked like she was a mermaid under water, but her physique seen out of the water was that of a human. Her hair turned blackish brown above water, but her hair under water was still light blue. It looked like a miracle and her presence was extremely powerful. Her skin tone was fair, but not white. She had baby pink lips and they were the most beautiful lips a human being could ever have.

The strangest part was that she already had earrings. It looked as if she was completely dressed. She had a pendant comprising a single large beautiful pearl, and wore a cute blue top and a pair of blue jeans. She was almost out of water. As she walked out, she saw that she had sandals on. It all looked awkward, but she knew everything about humans and human lifestyles. She was definitely well prepared. It was proved by this. There was still something normal: she was wet. Everything around her looked extremely pleasant. Along with her beautiful shells, she came along. Her transformation was like an angel coming out of water.

As she came out, before she opened her eyes, an aura was clearly seen. She opened her eyes and took a deep breath. That aura merged into herself. She swiped her hand over her hair and took a deep breath and in just a few seconds, the water evaporated. Her wet clothes were completely dry, but the fact remained that she really was upset. She looked around and noticed her legs. She removed her sandals so she could feel the sand under her foot. She did enjoy it and smiled after a very long time. She had brown eyes and the length of her hair remained the same. It was really long!

She was about 5 feet 6 inches tall and a slim girl. She was confident and smart but looked innocent at the same time. It was 5:45 AM by then. Nature celebrated her presence and the atmosphere was cool and calm. She was missing Yara, and this was very obvious on her face.

She said emotionally, "I really miss you Yara!" She looked shocked and said, "Did I just call her name out?" It was the first time she spoke in the human world and it put her in shock! Mermaids never called each other with names. This was the first time she called her Yara instead of Sakhi! She realized what the King mentioned, and said to herself, "Oh yes! The King mentioned behaving like a human and being a human. Hmmm. I hope everything goes well!" She was trying to self-answer all her questions as nobody else could do that for her. She wore her sandals again and was about to leave.

Immediately then she heard music, and looked around. On her left, a few youngsters had begun playing the guitar and were singing. They were just having fun. She found it attractive as she loved music and went closer to them. She was quietly listening to the music. Then, they suddenly stopped playing. She found it very weird and thought maybe they didn't like her presence. She said, "Oh, I'm sorry, guess I shouldn't be here, shall leave!" She turned. A guy among them was playing the guitar. He stood up and stopped her, saying, "Oh no! You misunderstood! We just stopped, looking at you! You look different, I mean nobody would just come here and stop and you're so beautiful!"

She was surprised that it wasn't that weird and said, "Thank you! You all play very well!" Another girl said, "So do you want to join us? We play here every Friday, just for fun! So you can come, I'll introduce you to all of them!"

She began pointing out and calling their names. "I'm Tracy!"

Then, pointing at the guy who stood up first, "He is Kevin and my boyfriend and she, is Amanda, our friend!"

Amanda greeted her saying, "Hi!" The younger mermaid said, "Hi, nice to meet you guys! I would love to listen to you guys play. I almost forgot to introduce myself! I'm Nixie!"

Kevin said, "Beautiful! I mean, beautiful name!"

Amanda said, looking at Tracy, who didn't love Kevin's behavior, "Kevin you have to be careful, Amanda is right beside you!"

They were all standing. Tracy stood with her hands folded. Nixie thought they were in true love and said "Aww! So you guys truly love each other! Where did you'll find each other?

How did you realize you were in love?" Nixie asked all this out of curiosity without thinking what impression she might have been creating on them.

Amanda laughed and said, "Which world do you come from? We're only eighteen now! No serious yet, love needs time and space both, we're just getting to know each other!"

It seemed like things weren't fine between Tracy and Kevin. Nixie understood and made a decision. "Alright, you guys continue! I have to go now. It was nice meeting you all. Tracy, Kevin, you guys look great together!"

Tracy smiled and so did Kevin. They looked at each other and Tracy was blushing. Amanda thought Nixie was a smart girl. Nixie left saying bye and they all said bye. Then, they started playing the guitar.

After walking a distance on the beach, Nixie began talking to herself. " So this is how it works! God knows how I will be able to find true love. I don't believe I just lied! They don't look great together. They don't even love each other! Gosh! This world!" Saying this, Nixie walked out of the beach. As she walked by, she suddenly stopped and turned around. Looking at the beach with tears in her eyes, but then took a deep breath to overcome her emotions. This proved that Nixie was not happy, but was trying to pretend that she was happy because she was aware of the fact that sad faces don't gain attention.

Nixie was on the main road. Looking around with the thought of grasping everything she could set her eye on, she noticed human activities and their actions and reactions. It was like magically grasping and understanding everything. She had a major question. "God! I have to find a place to stay!" She was in the middle of the road and a car was about to dash her, but she stopped a second ago. Nixie was stunned and ran away as lots of cars were messed up because of her! She finally stopped on the footpath and said, "Oh, I was almost dead!"

She closed her eyes and found a place where she could stay. Nixie was excited and said, "Found it!!" She was so loud that everybody around looked at her. She tried explaining, but it didn't work much. "House? Where I can live? I mean come on!"

She was trying to explain it to people around her, but soon, she got fed up and just walked the wrong way. After walking for some time, she realized that she was walking in the wrong direction. She started walking in the right way. She was innocent and stupid at times. Nixie stopped a taxi and sat inside. She magically got a visiting card with the house address and gave it to the taxi driver and finally relaxed.

Nixie stressed about the sudden happenings. Nixie looked around and out of the window. She was smiling as she looked around. She looked up high into the sky and wished that she succeeded in finding that guy soon. She noticed people, shops, malls, kids, aged people, towers and cars, and almost everything there was to see, very precisely.

Nixie then murmured, "Hmmm, cars are better, I should try them!"

The taxi driver politely asked, "Ma'am, may I ask you something?"

Nixie replied, "Sure!"

The taxi driver said, "Your perfume smells great! Which brand is it? I want to buy a present for my girlfriend!"

Nixie was surprised because she did not use any perfume. But, she still managed an answer, awkwardly at that. "Well, actually I got this as a gift! I don't know which brand it is!"

The taxi driver casually said, "Oh, ok!"

Nixie then thought, "Perfume? I did not use any perfume! Strange!" The taxi driver thought that it was a perfume and Nixie was confused. It was naturally in her. Soon, they reached the bungalow and Nixie got off, and magically generated money just by opening her fist. She paid the bill. The taxi left and Nixie stood right before a huge bungalow in one of the best locations! Nixie walked ahead to the main door of the bungalow. There were three bungalows in a series.

Nixie noticed the lock. She smiled, looked at her hand. The keys appeared on her palm. She opened the door and got in. As she closed the door behind her, she heard a playful sound. She looked around and found a little boy and a man playing basketball. She was impressed by looking at the love they had between them. Nixie murmured, "They have such a strong bond between them! Finally, it felt like there is love between people out here!"

Nixie moved on. She stood still on the patio, looking at the bungalow and thinking about something. Nixie began talking to herself and dramatically said, "Hmmm, now where do I go? I really wish that my true lover magically appears in front of me and then immediately falls in love with me! Then I'd break his heart, he'd cry, I'd collect the love tears and bring Yara back to life! Simple! Just listening to this sounds so simple. But this doesn't seem simple to do! Hmmm, anyway, after I've turned into a human, I've become really mean! I do not like all this at all!"

Nixie took a deep breath. She was definitely upset and was not able to decide that what she should be doing next. After all, she was trying her best to get over it and focus on the reason why she was in the human world, and decided that she had to remain happy. Nixie was going through really complicated mixed emotions. While Nixie opened the door to the bungalow, she inserted the keys in the lock and said, "I miss you Yara!"

Nixie had wet eyes and tears rolled down her cheeks. She wiped it gently. She tried her best to act normal. The moment she got in the house, a basketball hit her on her head and she spontaneously exclaimed out loud, "Aaooo! Human life is really painful!" She was shaken for a few seconds and then heard a mature male voice saying, "Oh God! Are you fine? We are extremely sorry!" Nixie peeped in. It was her neighbor and his son whom she had noticed before.

Nixie exclaimed, "It's okay! I'm fine, my head is spinning a little but I am sure I will be fine soon! Don't worry!"

Her neighbor and son came running to her bungalow and her neighbor said, "We are so sorry! It's my fault! I threw the ball in the wrong direction, so sorry!"

Nixie thought he was really worried, so she casually said, "Oh no, don't be so sorry, it's okay!"

Her neighbor said, "Anyway I'm Jackson Martin and he's my son Sam and you are?"

Nixie said, "Nixie, I'm the new tenant here! I just shifted and my luggage is on the way."

Sam interrupted, "Okay! So you will be here for long? That's great! We can be friends! I mean, after all I have friends of your age! No one is my age. I live with dad so you know, I'm a man!"

Sam seemed to be a very confident, but just not for his age. He was very charming and his dad looked like a middle-aged, decent man. Sam's dad was used to all this behavior of

Sam's and he knew how talkative his son was. Nixie said, "Oh that's amazing! We're friends from now!"

Sam said, "Yes we are! Hey, today's my birthday!"

Nixie said, "Wow! Happy birthday! How old are you now?"

Sam said, "I'm ten now! Isn't that like a man? Just a few years to go, so I can officially be a man! I have a party tonight by 8:00 PM. Do come, we'll be waiting!"

Nixie happily said, "Your kid is incredible, don't worry I'll be there!"

Sam said, "People, please excuse me. I have to pee. See you at the party then! Bye!" He ran into his house. Nixie and Jackson laughed and admiringly said, "It's great that you manage time for your son!"

Jackson's face fell a little and he said, "Well yes! I'm a single parent. My wife passed away when Sam was five, and I thought of mentioning this because I wanted to let you know. Please avoid talking about Sam's mom."

Nixie sadly said, "Oh, don't worry about that! I won't mention anything that could ever hurt him!"

Jackson smiled and said, "Thanks, I have to go now. You take care and let us know if need any help and do come in the party, it's at the Martin's!"

Nixie said, "Is that yours?"

Jackson smiled. "Yes it is!"

Nixie said, "Oh great! I will be there!" Jackson said, "Okay then, bye!" Nixie said, "Bye!" Both waved hands and Jackson left. Nixie seemed to be happy and walked into the house. Nixie was highly shocked looking at the condition of the house. It was a huge mess and extremely dirty! But then, she did magic and lifted her hand high. Her finger tips were sparkling. She clapped and things started to fix themselves on their own.

Chapter 4

Nixie's Transformig Feelings

On the same day, William and Billy were at racing practice on one of the top most racing tracks. Both of them wanted to win. Louis, Kat, Leonax and Anne were cheering them, standing on the side stands. Louis was in a mechanic's suit. He looked dark and was over thirty. He was charming. Kat, Leonax and Anne looked like they were in the same age group. That was about twenty.

They were well-dressed and were snooty towards Louis. Louis stood alone. Kat, Leonax and Anne formed a group. William won the practice race and this is why Kat, Leonax and Anne's face went down. They didn't look happy about it. Louis was happy and cheerful. The moment William and Billy's car stopped, William ruffled his hair and looked confident about winning the racing jam. Billy looked a bit under-confident but was arrogant as usual.

Louis congratulated William saying, "Good game, William! Seems like someone is frustrated!" Louis was picking on Billy. Kat, Leonax and Anne were busy around Billy, giving him energy drinks and a towel. It looked dumb. William and Billy walked close to each other and the rest followed them. William looked tired but was charming. Billy was extremely tired.

William looked cool and calm. Billy was grumpy and filled with attitude. William casually said, "It seems like you are tired in the beginning itself!"

Louis laughed and looked at William. They high-fived and Billy arrogantly said, "You know what?" William nastily said, "What?"

Billy said out of the frustration of losing, "We'll see in the final racing jam!"

William and Louis were so used to all this that they just did not hear what and how he said it. Billy nastily said, and in a very teasing manner, "Look girls, who's laughing! Louis, who is thirty and yet a car mechanic, at least we are all in our twenties!"

Louis found it very offending. So did William, because both were great friends. William was grumpy and said, "You!" Louis stopped him halfway. Louis said, "Correction! Head of the car mechanic team. At least I have my own earnings and I don't beg around anybody for money, just like you beg around your dad. He earns and you spend!"

William and Louis exchanged mischievous looks. William said, "Forget it Louis! Let's focus more on cars than on girls!"

Billy interrupted, "Girls fall flat for me! You're jealous or what?"

William made fun of him. "Girls fall flat for you! Hahaha, joke of the day!"

Then William walked closer to Leonax, Kat and Anne and just to taunt Billy he played all this drama. "Hey girls, how are you all doing?" He was flirting dramatically!

The girls were overwhelmed by this and began making noise, saying, "Oh my God! I don't believe it, you really mean by us, this is the best day of our life!"

William looked at Billy, "I'm not into girls for now! Good for you!" Billy was irritated and just failed to turn the situation like he wanted. Louis said, "At least teach these glue girls something! Their reactions remain same in all situations, whether good or bad!" Then, he made a funny face and said, "So Mr. Showoff, at least have something real!"

Billy was annoyed and said, "Shut up!"

Louis dramatically said, "I'm not pulling up my shirt up here!"

William and Louis laughed, Billy was grumpy and the girls were silent.

William casually said, changing the topic to Louis, "Let's leave now! We're getting late. Remember Sam's birthday party! He's going to kill me if I am late again and I also have to buy a gift for him, will you come along?"

Louis said, "No, I already bought one for him!" In the meantime, Billy left in a huff and his girls' team followed him like dumb puppets!

William and Louis laughed and went on their way. It was almost six in the evening. Nixie walked into a mall. She seemed excited and surprised as she looked around. The mall was bright with lots of light. There were too many people around and Nixie was busy noticing them. For her, it was an all-new experience of life. Nixie casually said, "Mission gift for Sam!" She had come to the mall to buy a gift for Sam. She looked around and then decided that she would take the escalator so that she could look at all the people around in the mall.

While she walked towards the escalator, she noticed a couple fighting. The husband was trying his best to convince his wife saying, "Come on sweetheart, can we please get this fight to end now?"

The wife aggressively said, "Oh no, you go hang out with your friends no matter where I am!"

The wife walked out of the mall and the husband was left embarrassed. Later, he also walked out of the mall. Nixie was noticing them and she was very confused because she couldn't understand why the couple was married if they still had no understanding. She was also stressed about it. If this was how it works, she would never be able to find true love! Nixie said, "Wow! What a strange thing love is! I mean, if this is how it works then I'm in big trouble!"

Nixie reached the escalator and noticed a boy and girl holding hands and stood together on the escalator. They were extremely lovey-dovey and shared a few kisses on the cheeks. The boyfriend said, "You know, I love you so much!"

The girlfriend said in the same tone, "I love you too!" They reached the next floor and walked out of the lift. Nixie was confused! She just couldn't understand what love was in the human world! She then said, "Was that really love? I doubt it!"

But, avoiding all that, Nixie went straight to the toy shop and suddenly stopped. She started feeling like something was happening in her stomach. She was starving! She soon realized that it was due to hunger and said, "I think I'm hungry!" Nixie was excited that she would eat food just like humans do. Nixie went to the food court and looked around, gazing at things and people.

She then went to one of the counter and stood in the queue, she was looking around. As soon as her turn came, before the guy could ask her anything, she said "I'll have a vegetarian cheese pizza with tomato ketchup!" She was spontaneous. The counter guy wasn't surprised because a lot of people behaved that way. Nixie had to pay the bill. She used magic and found money in her pocket. Nixie waited there for the food.

After she got it, she found a vacant table and settled down. She soon finished eating. While wiping her mouth, she smelled something foul. She turned around and there was a man taking fish to his table, Nixie was shocked and couldn't see it. She was naturally concerned as she belonged to the marine world. Nixie was grumpy although she knew that this was a very common thing on part of humans. She realized that knowing something is one thing and practically seeing it happen is a totally different thing. Nixie stood up from her seat and tapped the man's shoulder. The man casually turned around and said, "Yes?"

Nixie said emotionally, "How could you?"

The man found it very awkward and said, "Sorry, I didn't get you!"

Nixie took a step back in shock and she felt like it was all creepy. Nixie was in tears. Everybody looked at them. The man was also feeling awkward as he couldn't understand what Nixie was talking about. He was worried that people were probably misunderstanding them.

The man humbly said, "Madam, whoever you are, I'm not getting you at all and I guess people are misunderstanding us!"

Nixie was least bothered at what everybody around was thinking of them. She said in the same tone, "You can't understand how important it is to me! It makes no sense explaining all this to you!" She left, wiping her tears.

The man was embarrassed and loudly said, "Come on people! I don't even know her! I don't know what she was talking about! I'm engaged!" The man immediately moved to another table.

Nixie was on the escalator going downwards. She was in a dilemma because she wasn't able to understand her own behavior. It was for the first time that she was grumpy and yelled at somebody. She indulged in her usual habit and started talking to herself. She had self-generated questions and self-generated answers.

She said, in feeling a little confused, "I don't understand why I yelled at that man. I knew that humans eat marine animals. Then why? Ahh!" She walked out on the escalator and went to the toy shop. She was still confused. "Maybe it's about the exposure of all human emotions! This is going to be complicated because as a mermaid, we did everything our way and everything was so clear! There were no complications but the human world is just the reverse, I know and understand human culture but I'm so not able to fit in, somebody help me!"

As Nixie got into the toy shop, she looked around, trying to figure out what Sam would like as a present. She looked at the toys. She was extremely confused as she had never done this before. Nixie said, "Hmmmm, let's see!" She tried to select a couple of things. But she wasn't able to stick to one. There was a salesman at the toyshop. He was looking at Nixie since the time she entered. He looked keen and sharp! He had no pure thoughts for Nixie! Nixie picked up a car and started feeling creepy because of the vibes from the salesman. She turned around for no reason and noticed the man at the counter but avoided him. After she selected the gift, she stood in the queue for payment and to get the gift wrapped.

Nixie waited for her turn. William rushed into the toy shop. He quickly selected a gift and stood in the line to get it billed. He stood behind Nixie. Nixie had left her hair loose and it was unusually very long!

William was admiring Nixie's hair and tapped her on her shoulder. "Hey hi!"

The moment Nixie turned, William was in love with her. Nixie was very genuine when she said, "Yes? Tell me!"

William smilingly asked, "What?"

Nixie awkwardly said, "You had tapped me. Do you want to say something to me?"

William quickly said, "Yeah! Is your hair real?"

Nixie smiled, "Yes they are!"

William said, "Gorgeous!" He wanted to continue the conversation, but he couldn't as it was already Nixie's turn. Nixie asked, "Get this wrapped!"

Sales guy said, "Sure!"

While the guy was busy wrapping the present, he continuously looked at her. Nixie wasn't okay with it, but without saying anything, she stood still. After paying the bill and getting the gift wrapped, she noticed the sticky tape holder and smiled mischievously. She picked up her belongings and the tape holder. She stamped the holder on his fingers and said, "Oops!" Then, she left. The guy learned his lesson well! William noticed all this and laughed. Nixie and William exchanged looks. William admired her and Nixie was casual. Nixie was walking and tripped, but William held her hand and saved her from falling down. Nixie did not realize when her pendant had gotten hooked with one of the toys and broke.

Nixie said, "Thanks, I don't know how I just tripped!"

William said, "That's okay!" Nixie left. After William paid the bill, he noticed Nixie's pendant on the ground down. He picked it up and looked for Nixie but she had already left. William ruffled his hair and said, "She was beautiful!" He walked towards the elevator and was continuously smiling and thinking of Nixie. William was waiting in the queue of the cars to exit and the car ahead of his was Nixie's. There was also a car ahead of Nixie's. William thought of Nixie and he found it strange that he was thinking of a girl for the first time. He realized that there was something really special in her and wished to meet her again and tell her how he felt about her. He wanted to give back her pendant. But that was just an excuse.

William had a way too much idea about what it feels like when you are in love. Because he was born as a human, unlike Nixie, who was transformed into a human, for her it was an all-new experience that she had heard of but was experiencing it for the first time ever. William thought and murmured, "Who was that girl? My heart skipped a beat for her! She was special, God help me meet her again!" Nixie's car moved to the toll booth and she was paying the parking charge. She put her head out of the window and asked the toll booth guy, "Excuse me, which way to the beach takes the least time?"

He replied, "Take the right!"

Nixie said thanks and moved on. William couldn't believe his eye. He paid the parking charges and chased Nixie. Nixie drove really well. William said, "This girl is furious and I love it! Thank you so much God!" Nixie reached the beach and parked her car. As she got out, she said, "I hope to feel better here!" She went to the beach and William arrived and parked his car. He chased her. Since he wasn't aware of her name, it was very difficult for him to stop her. He said loudly, "Hey you, stop!" Nixie did not pay attention.

He then said, "Hey you, with the long hair!"

She did not pay attention. She was busy looking calmly at the water and thinking about the past. She was a bit emotional. William did not lose hope and awkwardly said, "Hey you! Girl! It's you! The girl with extremely long hair!"

Nixie said, "Is that me?"

William suddenly and unexpectedly jumped before her and said, "Ya that's you!"

Nixie got scared and yelled, "Ahhhhhhh!"

He stepped back and said, "Oh, I'm so sorry!"

Nixie said, "No, that's okay! I know you, and we just met in the mall, right?"

William said, "Oh yes, so you remember!" Nixie then said, "I have to go, bye!" She turned around and moved on.

William chased her and said, "Hey, you have the most beautiful hair I have ever seen! Love youuuu…rrr hair!"

William was about to say 'love you', but looking at Nixie's expressions, he diverted his sentence to something else.

Nixie innocently said, not even thinking that William was flirting with her, "Thanks, you are really sweet!"

William was surprised because he was expecting cute or maybe smart and said, "Sweet?"

Nixie said, "Yeah!" William awkwardly accepted it, saying, "Oh ya, sweet!"

Nixie spontaneously asked, "Why are you following me?"

This was one of the creepiest and unexpected questions. William was shocked that anybody could be that sweetly and innocently blunt. He stammered a little in the beginning but then fixed his behavior saying, "Follow! I am not following you! Actually, yes, I was! I mean, your pendant fell down when you tripped, so I just wanted to return it!"

Nixie was so surprised. "Oh thanks a lot! I did not realize when it had fallen down! You came all the way to return my pendant! Thanks!"

William said, "That's like my job!"

William was trying to impress her whereas Nixie was absolutely clueless. "You are being paid for this!"

William said, "Oh no! I am a racer, this one's because I'm a responsible citizen and a good human being, that's all!"

Nixie said, "Oh, okay! Carry on! I have to go, bye!" She left. William was just waving hands. He turned around and excitingly said, "She's amazing! I should stay in touch. Oh my God! I should take her contact for that!"

He turned back to her but she left before he could reach her. William said, "My bad luck!" He looked at his watch and it was already 7:45 PM! William exclaimed, "Oh freak, I almost forgot! Sam's birthday party! I have to change, I'll be killed this time!" He rushed!

Nixie magically appeared with her car outside her bungalow. A man sat on the street. He noticed it. He was extremely drunk! He couldn't believe what he saw. Nixie was not aware of it and said, "Hmm, I'll be late! I should dress up here with magic!" Nixie used her powers and got ready in just a few seconds for the party. The drunken man yelled, "You are a magician! I'm not dreaming, it was real! I must trap you and keep you in a cage so that people will pay me so they can see you, I'll be rich!" Nixie yelled at the top of her voice and was stunned.

She ran inside the bungalow and closed the door. She stuck to the door and was panicking. She said, "Humans can be of all kinds! Oh God! If I keep behaving like this then I'm surely going to get into major trouble! I will not use any magic that people can see! AHHH! That means I have to drive a very long way!" Nixie sneaked out of her house and sat in the car. She started and noticed the drunken man behind the car through the mirror. Nixie said, "Oh no, not again!" She did some magic and left. The drunken man murmured, "What am I doing here?" It was memory loss!

Chapter 5

Beginning of Love

The Martin's was brightened. Many people got in with gifts. It was a huge, beautiful banquet with balloons and flowers as decoration. There were mostly lavenders and lilies, used with a purple and white combination of balloons. The birthday celebration was initiated with light music so that everybody could meet and greet each other. Sam was busy collecting gifts. He was constantly shaking hands and hugging people and said, "Thank you, thank you!" His cheeks were paining as he was smiling continuously for the past hour. He handed over all the gifts to one of the people in charge and asked his dad, "When is William going to come?"

Sam looked really desperate. He was rubbing his cheek over and over again. Before Jackson could answer, Billy walked in with Leonax, Anne and Kat. He was so dramatic and his girls were beautifully dumb like always. He immediately hugged Jackson and girls said together, "Hiii, happy birthday Sam!" He gave him the gifts. Billy said, "Hey, how are you?" Jackson said, "Great! What about you?"

Billy smilingly said, "All good!" Then, he noticed Sam and hugged him saying, "Happy birthday, boy!" and gave him the gift. Sam said thanks and looked as if he was waiting for someone special. Louis walked in and hugged Jackson and Sam and gave Sam his birthday gift saying happy birthday to Sam. Louis noticed Billy and said, "Ahh! Whose face did I see?" Billy found it offending and immediately reacted saying, "Did you just say something?"

Louis smiled sarcastically and was going to say something but Jackson interrupted. Sam was enjoying the nasty conversation between Louis and Billy. "Come on guys! At least spare each other for now!" Jackson said. Sam said, "But it's okay with me!" Jackson looked at Sam seriously. "Sam!" Sam realized that he shouldn't have said that but quickly made a puppy face and acted as if he was innocent. Jackson hugged Sam and ended the conversation. Billy noticed a group of girls and pulled his t-shirt up and said to the group, "Excuse me, I have to go, a girl group is waiting for me!" He left and his fans followed him.

Sam was still looking for William and was really sick and irritated of him being late all the time. He asked, "Where is William?"

Jackson was speechless and Louis said, "He's not yet here! Gosh! What does he do back at home?" Everybody laughed but Sam was so not casual about it.

Looking at Sam, Jackson tried convincing him for a while saying, "Don't worry, he'll be here soon!" Sam was still irritated, "But when? I've been hearing this for the past hour and more!"

Catherine walked in saying, "It's okay if my son is late. His mom is not that late!" Catherine was well-dressed and was aged. She was the mother of a young adult. She was charming and graceful. Sam smiled and so did everybody else. Catherine was just trying to distract Sam so he smiled! Catherine hugged Sam and gave him the gift, wishing him a very happy birthday! Sam thanked her. Catherine said, "William isn't here yet?"

They all had an idea of the drama that was going to happen! It looked as if Catherine was the principal and the rest were her students. It had nothing to do with age but they had so much respect for her!

William was going to walk in excitedly but suddenly stopped, looking at his mom! He was confused and pressed his eye in, like he knew what was going to happen next. He murmured saying "Oh God! Now which excuse should I use?"

He took a deep breath and made a decision. He then gradually walked in and excitedly and loudly said, "Hey mom!!"

Louis muttered, "And now the drama begins!"

Catherine was pretending to be grumpy and said, "How could you be so late, I mean always?"

William was thinking of a potential excuse and said, "Well, actually…"

Catherine understood that he was definitely hunting for an excuse. Catherine said, "I know the reason why you are late!"

William surprisingly said, "You know, really?"

Catherine said, "There are lots of possibilities. Maybe your car was punctured. You got it repaired. Or, you may have given a lift to someone lost or maybe a dog must have accidently come under your car and you took him to the hospital, or maybe it was very difficult for you to select a present for Sam which is why you are late!" Catherine pulled William's leg and William was speechless. Everybody was looking at Catherine but they didn't mind because they knew she was like that.

Catherine said, "In the past years, you have given all these excuses! What happened this year?" Catherine was definitely not serious and everybody else knew it.

William smartly looked around and said, "Mom! You have so many options, so choose what you like!"

Catherine laughed and said, "William!" William made a puppy face and it worked. They hugged and Sam said, "I am right; puppy dog face can fix any situation!"

Catherine was going to say something but Jackson interrupted and said, "Mrs. Thomas, forget it! William isn't the last person to come, Nixie has yet not reached!" Everyone heard that name for the first time. Jackson was going to explain, but before he could, Nixie walked in and said, "Hi! Happy birthday, Sam! I am sorry to be late. Actually, I'm kind of new to this place so wasn't aware of the roadways!" William was stunned. He couldn't believe his destiny! Jackson casually said, "It's okay but good seeing you here!"

Sam said, "Ya its all fine! Meet my friends! He is William!" Nixie excitedly said, "Hey you! We've met before! You drove all the way from the mall to beach to return my pendant!"

William pretended to be normal and said, "Yeah right! You? Here, how?" Sam introduced her and said, "She is my new friend!"

Sam's introduction was incomplete. Jackson said, "Our next door neighbor!" William said, "Ohhh, nice!"

Catherine said, "Finally, you were late for some new reason! Thank God!" Everybody laughed. Nixie didn't understand much, but smiled. William was feeling a little shy!

Catherine then asked Nixie, "Where are you from?"

Nixie spontaneously said the truth. "Not one place!"

People around were confused and Louis said, "What does that mean?"

Nixie said, "Well, I mean, I was born in Canada then we moved to Finland when I was fifteen. Now I'm here in New York. But my parents are yet in Finland!"

Jackson asked, "You're here for some reason!"

Nixie lied. "Yeah, I'm here because I'm writing a book on New York City! So I am touring this place!"

Everybody exclaimed, "Great job!"

Nixie was thinking, "I don't know how many more times I will lie!"

They all then exchanged contacts. Sam asked, "Give me your contact details, and take everybody's contacts! We'll stay in touch!"

Nixie thought. Magically, a phone was in her hand. The rest thought she already had it. They exchanged contacts with Nixie. Billy noticed Nixie and wanted to throw his weight around. He smartly walked towards Nixie. He made space for himself and looked at Nixie saying, "Hey beautiful lady, my name is Billy!"

Nixie was annoyed and said, "Girl!" Billy didn't get her. "Sorry, what?"

Nixie said, "I'm not a lady, I'm a girl!" Everybody laughed and Billy thought ill of himself.

Catherine changed the topic and said, "People, you all have fun! I got to go now. Strict instructions from the doctor! Nixie, come home someday! We can have a good time!"

Nixie smilingly said, "Sure aunty!"

William was very happy and thought, "What I couldn't do for so long, mom did in just a few minutes! Women power! Love you mom!"

Nixie came very close to William's face, staring at him. William was lost in thought. Jackson and Sam were busy with the guests. Louis watched Nixie and William. He tried to gauge their future, their relationship and Billy was busy flirting with the girls. Soon, William realized that Nixie was so close to him. He smiled and Nixie said, very curiously, "What are you thinking?"

William immediately lied to cover the fact. "No, nothing!"

Nixie spontaneously and bluntly said, "You're lying! Anyway, forget it!" William was shocked for a second and looked at Louis. Louis lifted his eyebrow and smiled. William ruffled his hair and expressed that he liked Nixie! The DJ announced something and everybody turned to look at him, "Hey people! Any of the guests interested to come up here and sing, dance, show us what you got? Be a sport! So let's ask the birthday boy to choose!"

Sam was going to say something, but suddenly the lights turned off and it was dark. Jackson appeared right in the middle of the stage with the spotlight on him. He wished Sam a happy birthday and the music began. Everybody was surprised. Nixie looked extremely happy and William came close to Nixie. Everybody danced and celebrated.

William and Nixie danced together. Billy didn't like it and was highly frustrated. Sam chopped the cake and everybody sang the birthday song for him. William and Nixie hugged each other. Nixie was casual as she also hugged Sam. But, William had something else going on in his head. Soon, dinner was ready. They ate together and most of the guests had already left.

Sam said, "Hey people, its present opening time!"

Like every other year, Sam began opening gifts! He was hyped and said, "This was the best birthday ever. Now, it is time to open gifts! This year will begin with Nixie's present because she is my newest friend!" Sam opened the present which Nixie had given him. It was a remote control zero gravity car and Sam looked excited. "Thank you very much Nixie! It's amazing!" Nixie smiled and William was shocked and stunned. Billy noticed William and said, "You have competition! Even Nixie understands Sam well, don't be so shocked!"

William sarcastically said, "You don't know what I'm shocked about!"

Sam then said, "Now for William's present!"

He unwrapped William's present. After he did, he was extremely surprised and loudly said, "William and Nixie, you guys have extremely similar choice. I got the same present from the both of you!" Sam smiled and picked another present. William and Nixie looked at each other. William had an extremely loving feeling towards Nixie. William said, "We can be good friends, Nixie!" Louis suddenly jumped in between and said, "We are all friends now, what say Nixie, I'm Louis by the way!" Nixie smiled, "Nice! Yes we are friends!"

Sam was busy unwrapping presents. William received a call and moved to the balcony. Billy noticed William going to the balcony, so he also followed him. William was on the phone. The moment he kept the phone and turned around, he noticed Billy standing right behind him with hands folded. William said, "You?" Billy arrogantly said, "Well, actually, I have something very important to discuss. It is not very complicated! Just stay away from Nixie! Actually, she's a very smart girl and deserves a smart man. Get that? Just stay away!"

Billy was about to leave when William tapped him on his shoulder and said, "If she's a smart girl and deserves a smart man, then how can I stay away from her" saying this, he left. Billy was slow to understand and when he did, he was so aggressive and wild! He found it extremely offending and grumbled. "You! I won't spare you!" Billy walked out where most of the guests had already left.

William was already there and was talking to Jackson. Nixie, Sam and Louis were casually talking and Nixie said, "I should go now, it's quite late!"

Jackson smiled and said, "Okay, but do come home!"

William asked Nixie, "Hey shall I drop you home?" Before Nixie answered, Billy pushed William from behind. It was a hard push. For a second, nobody could understand what that was supposed to be, and why such rude behavior was warranted, suddenly. William understood why Billy hit him. Everybody looked at Billy with the only question, 'why?' on their mind. Billy arrogantly said, "No, you need not drop Nixie back home! I will do that for you, you womanizer!"

William was extremely angry. He did not want to create a mess because he knew Nixie would get hurt. "Oh really? You shouldn't impose your qualities on others!"

Billy said in the same tone, "Shut up, you bloody bastard!"

William got even more aggressive now. "You better mind your language!"

Sam and Louis looked at Jackson who interrupted the boys and said in a low and settled voice, "Guys, can you both just stop it now? We can discuss it later! Let the guests go!"

William tried to calm down but Billy remained arrogant. Billy's three supporters walked closer to him but he also treated them badly and ignored them. Louis and Sam stood by William. Nixie was still trying to understand all that was happening as she couldn't understand why they were fighting over her. Jackson looked at the guests and everybody understood that the party was over. In just a few minutes, everybody had left. Nobody was there except for Nixie, Jackson, Sam, William, Louis, Billy, Anne, Leonax and Kat.

Louis curiously asked, "What is going on between you both?"

Billy was frustrated. He wasn't able to take the words and was annoyed. "You don't fall between us, get that, you stupid car mechanic!"

By now William's anger had turned to rage and he couldn't bear his friend being insulted. "Hey you! Control your tongue! Otherwise, I won't be able control my fist, get that, you spoilt brat!"

Billy was not concerned with the impression he was giving Nixie. Keeping all thoughts and sensibility aside, he punched William and said, "Why, what can you do?"

William punched him back and said, "What can I do? You better not ask!" They started fighting on a very serious level. Jackson kept his hand on his head and Sam was confused! Nixie was lost in thought. Two happy looking people could create so much disaster! She was unable to understand human nature! She realized that all that was going on was somehow because of her and she needed to fall in to sort things out. She tried stopping them and said, "Stop it people! Enough!" Nixie had just jumped between them and mistakenly, Billy fist hit Nixie really badly. She fell on the ground. Everybody got alert and went to Nixie, asking her if she was fine, they were all worried and concerned including Billy. Billy did not come closer to Nixie because he was embarrassed and arrogant.

Jackson asked, "Hey are you okay?" Nixie said, "Yeah! I am!" Nixie got off the ground and hit Billy twice, and that too, very hard! Billy and everybody else was shocked because Nixie seemed a very delicate girl!

After Nixie hit him back, she said, "Balanced! You hit me, I hit you back, and how can you be so cheap?"

"Anyway, it was good being here. Thanks! Happy birthday again, Sam! See you guys later, bye!" She rushed out. Billy was embarrassed and shocked. He was unable to face anybody and just walked out in shame. His fans followed him as always. Sam and everybody else were really worried. Sam said, in a low voice, "Dad Nixie must have felt really bad!"

Jackson thought for a second and said, "Hmmm, yes! William, can you drop Nixie back home and make her feel better? Tell her not to worry much about the fight!" William said, "Sure! Don't worry about that! I'll take care, and she'll be fine. Sam, don't bother with this. Chill, okay?"

Sam smiled and said, "Yeah, I will!" William left. Then, Jackson said, "Louis can you wait for some time? We can all go together! I'll check with the luggage in the room and get it wrapped!"

Louis causally said, "Ya sure!"

Nixie was getting out of the main door when William yelled her name. "Nixie! Listen! Stop! I want to talk to you! Long hair, stop!" Long hair was a pretty funny way to address her. Nixie stopped.

William came closer and said, "Girl don't be on fire!"

Nixie was still not normal and said, "Say, I'm fine!"

William said, just like a gentleman, "Should I drop you home?"

Nixie innocently asked, "I do have a car, right?"

William casually answered, "Ya, you do!"

Nixie said in the same tone, "I know driving, right?"

William again said, "Yes, you do!"

Nixie then straightened her backbone and said, "Then why will you drop me home?"

William laughed. "You have a really good sense of humor!"

Nixie smiled. "Thanks, shall I go now?"

Nixie was set to leave. But William stopped her, saying, "No! I mean, it's really late now and you seem so grumpy, you hit Billy - what if you hit somebody else on the road? You will be needing me! So, to be on the safer side, I can drop you home!"

Nixie smiled and said, "You know how to convince people really well, I appreciate it!"

William smiled and said, "Does that mean it is a yes?"

Nixie said, "Yes, it does!"

William jumped up. He then settled as a gentleman. It was a really humorous transition. But Nixie said, "There is yet another problem!"

William asked, "What is it?"

Nixie said, "Where will I keep my car?"

William tightened his collar. He didn't actually have a collar, but it was just a gesture. He said, "No problem is too big a problem when I'm around!"

Nixie politely asked, "And how you think you can fix this problem?"

William smiled and said, "I love being insane and know that it's good for health. The more you laugh, the more fit you are, even you must try it. I am serious about this!"

Nixie was confused and did not understand what the correlation was. "Can you please make it a bit simpler to understand?"

William smiled and pulled out the key of the car that was plugged in. He gave it to the watchman, saying, "Park the car aside, we'll be back in a few minutes!"

Nixie was not able to understand such behavior. She left it, still confused. William said, "Now, will you get out of the car? Otherwise, I can help you with that!"

Nixie said, "No, I'm good! But where are we going?"

William looked at her, keeping his finger on his lips. He said, "Shuuuu! You will have fun, no more questions!"

Nixie wanted to know and ask more, but William just dragged her in and she looked happy. But, she wasn't able to understand the reason why she was happy. She thought it was maybe because William was really sweet. But there was definitely something else that William understood. Though Nixie wasn't able to understand, William liked Nixie's company and he knew it. But Nixie liked his company and didn't know it! It was surely the beginning of love!

Chapter 6

Know that You're in Love!

Nixie stood with closed eyes behind the hotel. William hooked her car to his sports car. After he was done, he exclaimed "Done!"

Nixie was desperate to open her eyes and see what was happening. She asked, "Can I open my eyes now?"

William sweetly said, "Sure, princess!"

Nixie promptly opened her eyes and she giggled, saying, "Oh my God! This is amazing! You really are intelligent! Triple thanks to you!"

William was surprised and asked, "Why triple thanks?"

Nixie smiled and said, "Well, that is because you fixed my car's problem, you are dropping me home and third because you called me princess! Thank you, its balanced now!"

William laughed but knew that Nixie was really innocent and asked, "What is this balance that you mentioned?"

Nixie smiled and said, "Well, when people do good or bad things for me, I do the same for them so that I can balance and make human life simpler!"

William admired Nixie and the way she said things. She was so innocent and clear on her ideas. William loved it and said, "So let's leave now?"

Nixie nodded. William opened the door for Nixie. Both of them sat in the car and left. After a while, when Nixie sat quietly, William initiated conversation, and said, "Well you hit Billy really hard! Good job!"

Nixie said bluntly, as if she was still irritated by Billy's behavior, "I did not hit him but just balanced what he did to me!"

William laughed and Nixie said under her breath, "Hmmm, I guess it's the beginning of going through all emotions!"

William couldn't understand what she said, so he asked, "What?"

Nixie again tried fixing her talk 'and said, "Oh no, nothing! I'm really sorry, it is all because of me that you and Billy had to suffer, and after all you guys are friends!"

William corrected Nixie and said, "No, no! Don't live under this misunderstanding. All that happened wasn't because of you. We aren't even friends. We are competitors and practice together and have mutual friends. That's why people think of us as friends but it's not that way!"

Nixie said, "Well, I get that now!"

William changed the topic and said, "So you live in Finland? Is your family in Finland? And what about siblings or are you the only child?"

Nixie said, "Ya. I'm the only child! You tell me something about your family!"

William thought for a few seconds and answered, "Well my mom is a single parent. My dad passed by in a car accident when I was just seven. You already know about my friends. I am a racer, that's my passion and I look after dad's business. That's all about me!"

Nixie asked, "You must be missing dad?"

William got emotional and had wet eyes and said, "Yeah I do miss him!"

Nixie consoled him and said, "You know what? Your mom loves you a lot!"

William said, "I know, but how do you know that?"

Nixie answered, "It is clear on her face. Your dad passed away in a car accident. Even then your mom did not stop you from being a racer!"

William was emotional and said, "Yeah. She never comes to see the races, although she's always in the same country!"

Nixie consoled William by keeping her hand on his hand and smiling at him. William wanted to forget this so he wiped his tears and smiled. He said, "Well, forget all this. I have a race in Sacramento. If you are able to come, do come!" Nixie answered, "Sure!"

Nixie was yet lost in thought. She wondered how she would be able to find true love. It was then when she noticed a couple of people passing by. They looked dark and had destroyed faces. They looked down at the ground and were walking.

Nixie focused on one of them. The lady stopped and turned around to see Nixie. She looked at Nixie and moved on. She was scary but Nixie wasn't scared at all, she was wondering why these people were walking like dead people. That was then when she realized. They may have been dead people!

Nixie wasn't sacred at all, but was curious to see if William was able to see them and asked, "William, what time is it?"

William looked at the watch and said, "It's quite late! It's midnight!" Nixie was worried because she knew it wasn't good travelling when ghosts were around.

But she was confused as she couldn't find a good excuse. She purposely dropped her handbag down and exclaimed, "Hey William can you please stop the car, my purse fell down!" William said, "Oh, I'll get that for you!"

Nixie immediately interrupted, "Oh no, I mean it's near so I'll get it!"

Nixie got off the car and a dead woman stared at her and William for long. Nixie bent down and used magic and protected herself, William and the car, it was like a shield cover! She picked her purse and got back into the car. By then, the female ghost who was staring at them appeared in front of the car. But as she tried touching the car, some vibes went through her and she yelled, "Ahh!" and fell down. William was frightened and said, "Did you just hear something? Like somebody yelled? I felt like someone was here!" Nixie understood that humans can hear sounds and feel ghosts around them and that it also scares them! Nixie smiled to lighten the atmosphere and said, "It must be an illusion, let's go now!" William was convinced and they moved on. Nixie began thinking again about when she would find true love. "When will I find that true love!" she said to herself in her mind.

Nixie spontaneously said, looking at William, "Do you know a good guy?"

William laughed and said, "Why? Are you planning to get married? Even I am a good guy!"

Nixie widened her eyes and was thinking, "God, I'm stuck again!" And then she said, "No, I mean!" Looking at William's expression, she burst into laughter and said, "I am looking for a driver and guide. I want to understand the culture of this place and the people here!"

William asked, "But why so precise?"

Nixie was then correlating to the lie, so she said, "Remember I said I am writing a book on New York City?"

William curiously asked, "But why New York City?"

Nixie stammered a bit and said, "Well, here in this city, I find people to be workaholics with busy lifestyles. This book is on how people are, will and should manage work and family!" William was impressed and said, "Very impressive!"

William said, "Well, I'm not a bad driver! I was born and bought up here, so I know about people and places, and for a long time, I haven't toured New York! I can show you around, only if you want, of course"

Nixie said, without delay, "Good idea! Okay then, thanks!" William was also happy now that he would get time to hang out with Nixie just like he wanted. He said, "It's always my pleasure!" William was really sweet to Nixie and was continuously looking at her. Nixie thought he was just being nice to her, but it was more than just being nice to her.

They soon reached Nixie's house and William said, "So, here you go!"

Nixie again said thanks and William casually said, "How many times will you say thank you? You don't have to!"

Nixie said, "Well as many times you do something good to me, I will express that I appreciate what you did for me!"

William said, "Very thoughtful!" He was admiring the kind of person Nixie was! He then said, "Anyway, from when do we start the tour of the city?"

Nixie said, "From tomorrow, if you're okay with it?"

William smiled. "I'm always okay with touring with you!"

Nixie smiled and realized that William had done quite a favor on her so courtesy was to offer food. This was why she suddenly asked, "Would you like to come in and have something?"

William said, "No, I'm full of food right now, but I'll come someday, I promise!"

Nixie said, "Promise is a very big word, make sure you do!" Both smiled casually.

William said, "So I'll pick you up by 10:00 AM!"

Nixie said, "Sure! See you tomorrow then! Bye, good night, take care!"

William said, "You too, take care!"

Nixie then walked into the house and William turned around to leave. He received Louis' call, he stopped right there and answered the call 'Hey, you've reached home?"

Louis was at home in the bedroom and said, "Yes I did, how is Nixie now, is she still furious?"

William said, "No, she's incredible! It did not even take much time to convince her! She's absolutely fine. You say?"

Louis said, "Cool! So practice tomorrow by 11:00 AM. Please be on time!"

William ran his hand through his hair and said, "Actually, I won't come for the next few practices, I'm showing Nixie around!"

Louis teased, "Hoooo! I get that brother! It's okay, you're a champ. For now, focus on your love story! I don't want to be the bone in the chicken!"

William liked it, but denied it nevertheless. "Listen, it's no love story!"

Louis said, "Oh shut up, I know what it is! Okay! Bye, now. I'm really sleepy! You carry on!" He hung up.

William murmured, "Hmm, who knows, maybe it is a love story!" He then left.

Next morning, when the sun was mild at about 9:00 AM, Catherine was busy making breakfast and talking to William. The kitchen was seen from the dining area in their house and this was how Catherine was talking to William in the kitchen. William was waiting for breakfast and thinking of Nixie and smiling all the time! Catherine was trying to make her son realize that he was in love and that he must accept it. "Why didn't you tell Louis that for the first time ever in your life, a girl has impressed you so much? It is the truth, you like her, isn't it?" William was shy and trying to hide his feelings for Nixie and said, "Oh mom! I'm just helping Nixie, that's all!"

Catherine came in the dining area with the snacks. While serving them to William, she said, "Shut up, you liar! If that is so, I'll help Nixie, you can focus on your race!"

William excitedly said, "No!"

Catherine smiled and both exchanged looks as if Catherine had caught William's feelings for Nixie. Catherine said, "Don't be so scared! I'm not going to fall in between and I'm going to Sacramento before your racing jam! My doctor will be there. I'll meet him and with that, my treatment is done. You will be there for the racing jam? Then I'll return with you all!"

William said. "Okay! And if you already knew everything, how I feel about Nixie then why did you ask?"

Catherine laughed and said, "Now you're saying the truth! Anyway, I liked her from our very first meeting. She is a nice girl! You have made a brilliant choice, I'm so proud!" William acted like he was just concerned with the breakfast but he was carefully listening and smiling. Catherine said, "If you bring her home as my daughter-in-law, I'll be in seventh heaven!" William exclaimed happily, "Mom!" Louis knocked the door and Catherine opened the door. It was no surprise - it was routine. Louis sat next to William and Catherine began serving Louis.

William was almost done eating and Louis said, while eating, "You didn't tell me that you're marring Nixie, I just heard!"

William was taking a bite but stopped halfway and said, "Ya, it was just you who was left to pull my leg on this topic and now both of you tease me together!"

Catherine said, "You can't hide it from us! Louis is like my son. I also said that if you can't bury my dead body, Louis can and that's a major responsibility!"

William turned grumpy and said, "Why do you always have to talk about death? I'm going now!"

Catherine again teased him saying, "To get my daughter-in-law!"

William smiled and said in the same tone, "Oh come on! Don't start again, I'm leaving, bye, both of you!" He left, taking his car keys.

Catherine and Louis were left laughing. They had breakfast and Louis casually said, "Aunt, know what? I think William must marry Nixie, she's a good girl!"

Catherine seriously said, "And you?"

Louis said, "I don't want to marry Nixie, I'm serious!"

Catherine said in the same temperament, "Don't act smart. I'm not talking about Nixie. You must marry somebody!"

Louis looked upset and said, "Marriage for me is impossible! You know how much my little sister - my life - cried because of a heartbreak! I'm really scared of love! After Jazz committed suicide and mom and dad died out of cancer, I find my life very hopeless! Can't put myself at that spot!"

Catherine said, "Life is never hopeless! You can always have a chance!"

Louis was emotional and said, "No aunt! I'm already thirty-five and I've found you and William, that's more than enough for me!"

Catherine was trying to convince Louis. "But-" Louis cut her midway and said, "Oh aunt! Don't worry. But you have to promise me that the both of you will always stand by me!"

Catherine smiled and said, "You don't even have to say that!" Both had tears in their eyes but smiled. Catherine walked to Louis and hugged him. Louis wasn't Catherine's son but they had an amazing strong bond. For Louis, Catherine and William meant his life.

William had reached Nixie's bungalow and stopped his car in front of it. He fixed his hair and was getting ready like he was going for a very special date. He looked a bit nervous. He walked out of the car and yelled, "Hey Nixie, I'm here! Nixie, anybody home!" Then, he realized that he shouldn't have yelled so much. "Oops! I shouldn't have yelled!"

Nixie came out into the balcony and said, "Yeah, I'm coming!" She said it with tremendous energy! William was surprised by her expression and murmured, "Wow, she wasn't irritated at all!" Nixie reached down by then and was carrying a bag with her. She locked the door and walked out. Without saying anything, she kept her bag on the back seat and then said, "Hi, good morning! Let's leave!"

William couldn't get his eyes off Nixie and said, "Sure, you are looking great and different!"

Nixie and William sat in the car. William opened the door for Nixie and then he sat down. Nixie said, "Yeah. I was too bored yesterday so I watched TV, a fashion expert's interview. She was talking about how important it is to change our clothes according to occasion! There is just too much for humans!"

She innocently said this. William couldn't understand much and said, "Humans?"

Nixie then realized what she said, and tried fixing her words saying, "I meant girls!"

William smiled and curiously asked, "And you didn't already know this?"

Nixie was stuck again. She felt really stupid. "Of course I knew it! I was just kidding, before I came here, I prepared a lot to know everything about humans!"

William was extremely shocked and said, "Again humans?" Nixie again backtracked and said, "I meant Americans!"

William casually said, "There is not much difference in the basic fashion sense I guess!"

Nixie thought was some time and said, "I believe in micro minute detailing!"

William asked, "Nixie what are you saying?"

Nixie mumbled, "When I find out, I'll tell you!"

William asked, "Did you just say something? Why are you behaving little weird today?"

Nixie felt stupid of and said, "A little? Are you sure?" They laughed. They were about to leave when Jackson stopped them saying, "Hey, so you guys are set for the New York tour?" William and Nixie were both surprised to see him. William said, "Yeah, but how do you know this?" Jackson said, "Your mom!"

William smiled and Jackson whispered into William's ear, "Don't worry, I'm not here to interfere in you love life!"

William spontaneously asked, "Even you know that?" Jackson said, "Of course, I mean Sam was jumping after hearing this!"

Throughout the conversation, Nixie wasn't able to hear a single word and then she was really irritated and said, "People, even I am here, tell me what you guys are talking about!"

William nastily looked at Jackson and said, "Tell her!"

Jackson said aloud, "I'm here to invite you both for the inauguration of my new hotel on New Year's Day! I'll text you the address so I want the both of you to plan things accordingly. Okay?"

William and Nixie nodded and William said, "Mom?" Jackson said, "I know! She's going to Sacramento, no worries, you guys come!" Both smiled and Nixie and Jackson said, "You guys carry on, I got to go, see you all later!" Nixie and William said, "See ya, bye!" Jackson sat in his car and left. Nixie then asked William, "Where are we going first? I have a list of places I want to see!"

William took the list. After he read it, he threw it away. Nixie was expressionless. She didn't understand William's act and then William said, "Surprises are better! I promise in just 15 days, you will get this city very well! Leave it to me and no questioning! Okay?" Nixie smiled and nodded and William started the car and they left!

Every day, they had the same routine. They caught up by 10:00 AM and came back late at around midnight! They'd hang out all the time together and Nixie wrote her experiences in a book to justify her reasons that she had mentioned, which was why she came to New York.

While they were together, Nixie almost forgot about her task - the real reason she had come to the human world as a human. But it was alive in her unconscious mind. Sometimes, she used to get emotional when she used to think of Yara. William had noticed this sudden change in Nixie's behavior but they avoided it for some reason or the other. In just 15 days, they had visited the New York skyline where Nixie was wondering how huge and unique the human world was! She was lost in thought, thinking that humans have everything with them but were still not peaceful. Just the thought of Yara and her task used to disturb her, but she also used to forget it soon because of William's company. They saw Times Square where they shopped. William was busy carrying shopping bags and was very keen on making Nixie feel extremely comfortable. He'd wear funny masks and crack jokes to make her laugh. They saw museums where Nixie was lost in old cultures and history and was trying to correlate the past and present.

They visited the Bronx Zoo. Nixie was familiar with the animals and William was impressed looking at Nixie. It seemed as if Nixie was able to talk to the animals and react to their activities. It was understood when a tiger walked near Nixie. Although he was in an enclosure, everybody was scared when he roared. But Nixie went close and touched him. Before the guards came in to stop her, she took her hand off and the tiger seemed to be crying.

They talked for a while and then Nixie said to the guards, "There is something wrong with the tiger!" The guards said, "He isn't doing well these days! Probably a health problem! The doctor will be coming tomorrow!" William looked at Nixie. She used her powers to treat the tiger and in just a few seconds and he was alright and fit. Everybody was shocked, Nixie pampered him and then he bent down on his knees and bowed Nixie! Nixie smiled and then moved on. William asked Nixie, "You are an animal lover I guess!"

Nixie said "I am a nature lover!" William was impressed. They had food together and were really sweet to each other. Nixie had such a strong aura that wherever she went, people complimented her for some reason or the other - sometimes for her beauty, eyes and most often, for her hair. Then saw the dignity of the Statue of Liberty and clicked pictures everywhere they went. They also visited Staten Island, and sat together on the ferry.

It was very romantic but Nixie had no idea that it seemed more like dating. William was in love with Nixie by now and then they went on to the Brooklyn Bridge. Nixie looked at the water without even blinking. She was upset. Then, she looked up at the sky and noticed a shooting star. She told William about it. They both made a wish. Nixie closed her eyes and wished, "I wish to find the true lover very soon and make everything alright!"

William wished without closing his eyes, "I wish Nixie loves me exactly the way I love her! I really want it to be true love!" After they made their wishes, they looked at each other and smiled. Both their smiles were saying something. Nixie was thankful for everything that William did for her and William was in love with Nixie! They saw a few more places including Coney Island where Nixie became a kid on the rides. William was happy because Nixie was happy. They had snacks and William went to wash his hands while Nixie waited.

An old aged couple was leaving and before they did, the lady told Nixie, "You are very lucky to have such a boyfriend!"

And her husband said, "He really loves you, don't let him go, you both look and happy and great together, God bless you both!" They left. Nixie was stunned and speechless because she never thought that William could be the true lover she was in search of. She was messed up with a lot of thoughts. William came back and they both left.

They had reached Nixie's house. Nixie got off the car. William asked, "So here we end the tour, did you have fun?"

Nixie excitedly said, "It was incredible and it was fun all because of you, I just can't thank you enough!"

William said, "I promise, I'll always be there for you, whenever you need me!"

They exchanged intense looks and William said, "If you want to rest tomorrow or work on your book, you can. We have to attend Jackson's hotel inauguration in Manhattan, so what say?"

William didn't really want to let Nixie be alone. But he was not sure if Nixie felt the way he felt about her. Nixie was in a dilemma, whether to say yes or no. She desperately wanted to be around William, but she thought maybe William wouldn't like it. So she said, "Okay, I will meet you day after, then!" They both said, "Okay!" Nixie said, "Bye, see ya, take care!" William said, "You too! Bye, goodnight!" Nixie was on her way back home and William drove to his home.

Nixie was back home and doing a regular job of keeping her outfits in the wardrobe just like other girls do. She almost forgot she could do things using magic and was thinking of William all the time. She just couldn't get him out of her head! The more she tried, the more she thought about him. She didn't know what was happening to her but she liked it! William drove to his place, smiling and thinking of Nixie all the time. He was confused as to whether Nixie loved him or not, but was sure that he loved her company.

His mom turned on the light and said, "My little boy is finally in love!" William smilingly said, "How do you know that?"

Catherine said, "Look at your face, boy! You're blushing! So tell me, did you both kiss!"

William thought for a few seconds and said, "No! We didn't! I guess she just doesn't love me!" Catherine dragged William and both sat on the couch.

And Catherine said, "I knew it!"

William asked, shocked, "That she isn't in love with me?"

Catherine giggled and said, "No! That's not what I meant! I know she is totally in love with you. Love isn't about kissing each other and just being happy and hanging out all the time together. It's a beautiful feeling. You have a responsibly to understand each other and stand by each other throughout life! Just kissing and fulfilling demands is not love. What if in time, two people don't kiss or they aren't able to fulfill luxuries? Will that mean love is now dead and they must break up?"

William was listening carefully and trying to grasp everything. "How does one know if they are in love or it's just a short term attraction?"

Catherine said, "William, love is beyond attraction! When you're in love, you don't look at anybody except for your partner and so does your partner. You don't cheat on each other and you don't be self-centered. You do everything your partner would like. You start thinking and caring about your partner. Love can't be one-sided. It can only exist if both people love each other. If you love your partner to be able to satisfy your needs, then it isn't love. True lovers don't stop loving each other in the bad times and they never break up! If your partner isn't treating you the way you like, then you are with the wrong person! Are you getting it now? Love is a treasure. You are lucky that you have found Nixie!"

William was emotional and said, "I really am, mom! I am waiting for the day when we confess our love. Thank you so much for everything!" They hugged each other and went to their bedrooms. William couldn't sleep easily and even Nixie at her place was really restless. William at least knew that he was in love. But Nixie was still trying to figure out whether she was in love or not. She had a very strong feeling that William could be the right guy.

But she was also scared if it proved to be the wrong person, then things could go wrong. She was missing William as she was addicted to him. She desperate wanted to talk to somebody and know that what she was going through was love. But she couldn't, because she had nobody around. She was in tears as she desperately needed and missed Yara! Nixie was lost in thoughts of William and the time they spent together. Finally, both slept soundly, thinking and dreaming about each other!

Chapter 7

An Undisclosed Feeling

The next morning Nixie and William woke up early and were restless. Nixie looked at the clock. It was 5:00 AM. She thought of getting ready and then leaving with William but realized that they weren't going today. William came down to the hall and looked at the car keys. He wasn't going to use them. Both wished to be around each other but failed to explain it to each other. Nixie watched TV and William left for his racing practice. Nixie was bored because she had nothing to do. Time passed and it was 12:00 PM. William was busy with his racing practice but couldn't get Nixie off his head.

Nixie was lying on the bed. She fell asleep while watching TV. Suddenly, she woke up and was being lazy and began talking to herself. She had several magazines around her! She said, "Hmmm, I'm really bored now, I am such a stupid person! Why did I say let's meet day after? Ahh, if William was here, I wouldn't have been bored but I don't know if William likes being with me!

Or is he doing all this because he promised me? I don't even know where that true love is! If this is how it's going to go on then maybe in the next few years I'll be able to find true love! What do I do now?" Nixie was extremely confused and was lying in a very awkward manner. She was bored with watching TV and reading magazines. She had finally made a decision and walked down to the patio. She looked around at the bushes, and thought of doing some gardening. She went back into the house and magically brought the tools and implements, seeds, water pump, saplings needed for gardening. She began gardening. She used fertilizers in the soil and made it appropriate for planting the saplings and seeds. She was done by the evening.

She was dirty all over but happy. She walked into the house and freshened up. She was restless and had nothing to do. It was 7:00 PM. By then, Nixie decided to cook. She was starving by then, and said, "I should cook!"

She went into the kitchen and magically, raw material required for cooking appeared right before her. She was confused, wondering about what to cook. She said, "I can cook with magic but I should try cooking myself like a regular human!" She had powers and she could have used them, but she wanted to know how it felt to cook. She referred a cook book that had hundreds of recipes. She picked a few and began cooking. She baked cakes and was busy with too many dishes. She had two hands and planned to cook as if she had six hands! As a normal human, she wasn't normal. This task she was busy with proved how special she was even without magical powers!

William got home from his racing practice.

Nixie was almost done with cooking. She spoke to herself, "When will I find true love? Even if I do, how will I understand it? Humans are so complicated, unlike mermaids! Humans have something else going on in their heads and speak something else! God alone knows where I will stand!" She missed William but just didn't confess to him.

William was in the backyard lying on the ground, looking up at the sky and the figures made by the clouds. He was thinking about Nixie and he thought it was Nixie's face in the clouds saying "I love you!" to him. It was just his imagination, and it broke fast when the clouds parted. Louis walked in and noticed William promptly and annoyingly changed expression. He first looked upset and then looked happy, but again changed and looked grumpy. He was smiling. He was going to change his expression, but Louis interrupted and said, "I don't understand what your future with Nixie is!" He lay down next to William. William looked at him and said "What do you mean to say?"

Louis was irritated and said, "Why don't you tell Nixie how much you love her?"

William was convinced. But he still faced problems and said, "I don't know if she feel's exactly the way I do, what if she doesn't?"

Louis began convincing him saying, "Listen man! I know what you're going through but you have to do something about it. She's alone at her place. If she is missing you then she loves you, very simple!"

William asked, "But how do I check if she's missing me?"

Louis felt sad for William and said, "I didn't know people will be dumb when they're in love!" William was still lost in thought and said, "I don't get you!"

Louis said, "I meant that you are dumb!"

William sat up straight on the grass. So did Louis. William said, "That's rude!"

Louis said, "Whatever! Go see her. Tell her that you are done with practice and that you thought of meeting her because you were passing by her home, don't tell her that you have all the way to see her!"

William asked, "But why?"

Louis said, "Do not use your brain! Get that, and now go!"

William said, "Thanks man, going!" He rushed.

Louis stopped him and said, "At least tell me what the faces you were making were supposed to be!"

William laughed. "Oh that! Well, I was upset because Nixie wasn't with me. I was happy when I knew I would be meeting her, but then became grumpy again, as I though she did not even stop me once to be around her. Then, I became happy again as those memories when we together came up in my mind."

Louis said, "Oh, very thoughtful! Man, you really are in love, now leave!"

William was running out when Louis yelled, "Sacramento Race on second January, don't forget!"

William yelled back, "No, I won't! Chill!" and went out. He took his keys on his way out.

Louis murmured, "I was never hot!" He laughed and yelled out, as he walked into William's house. "Aunty, I'm hungry!"

Nixie decorated the plates on the dining table and wondered if she should call William or not. She was confused about William's behavior. She thought that William was in love with her but she couldn't make a decision. Each moment she spent with William was running in her mind, brain and heart, and it was all involuntary.

Nixie wondered, "Should I call William for dinner? Oh no, he's got mom at home! Humans are so complicated!" She was in love. She wanted to spend all the time with William.

William was also in a similar condition. But somehow, they were playing hide and seek with each other's feelings. People around them understood that they had a lot of love for each other, but they were not able to accept that the feeling of love can be so sudden and unplanned!

Everybody knew that in the human world, people are selfish and self-centered. Nixie and William began thinking of each other as their first priorities. This was a change in both of them. For Nixie, it was way more important and a sudden experience in life. She had reached that stage of life where humans take years to reach. She had reached it in just a few days!

Nixie was busy thinking with the phone in hand. The door bell rang, it was loud enough to break Nixies thought process. She opened the door and was surprised by William's presence. She was really excited.

William said, "Hi!" Nixie hugged him. William was surprised by her behavior. He definitely loved it!

Nixie said, "Hi, I missed you much! Life is so boring without you. You know, I was going to call you because I cooked. Would you like to have dinner with me?" Nixie asked innocently. Nixie didn't try to fake it to make up her sentences at all, she spoke her mind out!

William said, "Slow down, girl! May I come in first?"

Nixie smiled and said, "Oh ya, sure!"

William got into the house. Nixie held his hand and both of them sat on the dining area. Nixie served food and it was too much for two people to consume!

William asked, "You cooked all this by yourself?"

Nixie smiled and sweetly said, "Yes I did!"

William said, "Girl you're a genius!"

Nixie served herself and sat on the chair. They began eating food and Nixie asked William, "How is it?"

William said, "It's delicious! Are you sure you cooked it?"

Nixie stopped eating and said, "What do you mean to say?"

William was just pulling Nixie's leg. He laughed and said, "Relax, I was just kidding!"

Nixie smiled and said, "I was never serious! Anyway, I'm planning to join a gym!"

William sulked and said, "What! Don't tell me that! Why? Do you wish to be invisible?"

Nixie laughed and said, "Hahaha! If I eat so much and such delicious food every day, I will have to join a gym!" They laughed. William understood she was just joking.

William complimented Nixie saying, "You are very different from other girls! You're a very genuine person!"

Nixie and William quietly looked at each other. Nixie said, "Thanks! You are great, too! I love being with you. You're not like Billy." She then mimicked Billy saying, "Hi! My name is Billy. You look beautiful, lady! Hahaha!" She then said, "I had to correct him saying it's not lady, I'm a girl!" They talked like they had never talked before!

They did not bother how late it was and were busy enjoying each other's company. They finished eating, but were still not done with their chat. Nixie's face glowed and William was charming. The more they talked, the more it seemed as though they were recharging themselves. They did not look tired. Nixie and William took their plates and kept them in the wash basin in the kitchen. They washed their hands.

It was 12:00 AM by then. They wanted to spend more time together. William said, "Nixie!"

Nixie turned around and asked, "Yes?"

William said, "Well, thanks a lot for such lovely dinner. I had a great time! I must leave now, you must be tired!"

Nixie answered, "Well, ya. Before you leave, we can go for a walk!"

William thought that maybe now Nixie is interested in him and said, "Ya sure!"

Nixie excitedly said, "I'll get my scarf!" Nixie went upstairs to her room, to get the scarf. She happily came downstairs, wearing her scarf. She looked at William closely. Her big doe eyes seemed extremely innocent. She was expecting a compliment from William. William understood that Nixie was looking for a compliment and this was why he purposely ignored her. He wanted to see her reaction when he did not compliment her.

Nixie said, "Hey, are you missing something!"

William pretended to think for about 30 seconds and said, "No, I don't think so!"

Nixie was humiliated and said like a little child, "I don't want to come with you, I wore a nice scarf and you did not even bother that!"

William felt like he was on top of the world and said, "You look gorgeous in whatever you wear, by the way purple is my favorite color!"

Nixie smiled and said, "Thanks!" Nixie was shy as she had bluntly asked William to compliment her. William did not react to her behavior but he loved that Nixie did care for his reaction, Nixie opened the door and they both walked out, Nixie locked the door and they left. Nixie and William were walking on the street. It was cold and they felt some awkwardness. William was in love with Nixie but was shy to confess to her. Nixie didn't know why she was so shy but she was definitely going through this emotion for the first time. Her thoughts stopped filling her head when William asked, "So do you like going for a walk?" Nixie got out of her awkwardness. She was back to her cool and calm self. Nixie had feelings for William but she avoided it every time. Nixie said, "Yeah. I like nature and everything that's pure!"

William smiled and he never let go of a chance to look at Nixie and admire her! He said, "Oh okay!" Nixie felt cold and her palms were very cold. She rubbed her palms together to feel better. William noticed it and held Nixie's hand. She was stunned and shaken for a few seconds, but then as William rubbed her hand, she calmed down. She felt better. William said, "Keep your hands in your pocket. You won't feel cold!" Nixie smiled and did what he said.

They walked for long together, without talking. They just looked around and sometimes exchanged glances and smiled. After walking a good distance and William spent a long time thinking in the process, he extended his hand to Nixie so she could hold it. William did this because he knew he was in love. Nixie did hold his hand, but her approach was really casual, as she considered William to be a very caring and protective true friend. She felt safe around William.

They had walked a long distance of about two miles. Then, they returned. The same thing continued. They were both speechless, but it was honestly a situation where feelings mattered more than words. Nixie was unknowingly in love with William and William knew that he was in love with Nixie. Nixie looked at her watch. When they reached Nixie's house, it was 1:30 AM. Nixie felt guilty as she thought that just because she had insisted, William had walked all the way with her, and that he probably was tired. But, he didn't tell her that. Nixie said to William, "I'm so sorry! I didn't realize it was too late, you must be tired!"

William smiled and said, "Don't be sorry! I loved walking with you and I must thank you for such a delicious dinner that you cooked!"

Nixie said, "Well, then it's balanced again, I guess!" They laughed.

William said, "Okay then, see you tomorrow, we will leave for Manhattan about eight in the morning!"

Nixie said, "Okay, see ya, good night and take care!" William sat in the car and said, "You don't want to go back in?"

Nixie said, "I'll go after you leave!"

William asked, "Why? You never did this before!"

Nixie innocently said, "I don't know. I just feel like doing that." William smiled and said nothing. He left and they waved hands. Nixie walked in, and soon, the lights were turned off.

Nixie and William gradually built a strong emotional bond. They had no give and take. They weren't doing anything out of the ordinary because Nixie was new to the feeling of love.

She had to find true love. William practically knew nothing about Nixie, but still loved her without knowing how rich she was or what kind of a family she belonged to. He didn't even know her last name. He had not even asked her much about her family and her past relationships.

There were things to come for Nixie and William, but they had built an emotionally pure bond and that was beyond any challenge!

It was another morning with a new beginning for everybody. It was 6:00 AM. Nixie, William, Jackson, Sam, Louis, and Billy all woke up. Nixie was up on the very first alarm sound, and so were William and Louis. Billy was lazy and hit snooze on the alarm. Jackson woke up earlier and was struggling to wake Sam up. Sam's sleeping bouts were next to never ending.

But somehow, everybody was ready by eight. They were busy adding finishing touches to their vacation look. Nixie looked at the mirror. Suddenly, she had wet eyes. She said, "I miss you, Yara! I hope to find true love on this trip and complete the mission. This is my priority for now. Till I bring you back to life, just like before, I won't stop!" Nixie left.

Nixie reached Jackson's place and the door was open. She knocked on the door and walked in and Jackson yelled from the bedroom, "Who is it?"

Nixie yelled back, "Nixie here!"

Jackson said, "Oh! Please sit on the couch, we're coming, sorry for the delay!"

Nixie yelled, "That's okay!" and sat on the couch.

William was tying his shoelaces, thinking of Nixie and smiling! Soon, he left, too. Billy dragged his huge luggage to his car. He dumped it in. He got a call on his phone and looked annoyed. He furiously kept the phone down and said, "I hate them! Useless people!" He sat in the car and left.

Louis was praying to God and said, "I wish Nixie and William always live happy and together, they deserve it, please bless them!" Louis also left.

William, Louis and Billy reached William's place at the same time and greeted each other. They walked into the house. At the same time, Jackson and Sam walked out, ready to leave.

They hugged each other and Louis asked, "So, Billy! Your three spoons aren't seen today! Did something go wrong?"

Billy grunted, "They are busy with their make up. They won't be coming!" Louis wanted to tease Billy, but Jackson stopped with a gesture! They left and sat in a big wide and spacious four-wheeler. They were excited, except for one person, Billy! He wasn't very happy about the trip! They were chatting, and then, the driver walked in. Jackson said, "Boy, you're late!"

The driver apologized and said, "I am extremely sorry, Sir!"

Jackson nodded in forgiveness and then they left. They were all in their own thoughts! Jackson and Sam were excitedly talking about their hotel series launch. They were all having fun. Louis was hoping for fun. He wanted to see William and Nixie together as a couple soon. Unlike Billy, who was of the totally opposite opinion.

He was jealous of William and Nixie, and did not like it when they sat next to each other and were super friendly to each other. Billy was obsessed with William and Nixie's break up. He wasn't even able to hide his negative feelings. It was clearly seen on his face! William couldn't think of anything except for Nixie! Nixie was hoping to find true love but her true love was right before her.

They played music and games in the car. They stopped at a restaurant for food. Everybody ate and the driver also sat with them. He wasn't left out although they did not interact much with him. They reached Manhattan and reached Jackson's hotel.

His hotel seemed huge and beautiful. The car went in and a few guards opened the doors of the car for them to get down. They were all happy. The treatment was like they were royalty. Their luggage was sent up to their rooms in the hotel and everybody walked into the hotel. There was a wide lobby with amazing seating arrangements. They looked around. Jackson was proud. Sam was also proud of his dad. Nixie then said, "This is beautiful, very peaceful, congratulations Jackson!"

Jackson smiled and said, "Thank you!"

William excitedly said, "Ya, it's amazing, congratulations!"

Jackson felt great. He smiled. Sam was having fun, running around and playing. He said, "Dad, this is too good, the best hotel!" Jackson hugged Sam and ruffled his hair.

Louis looked outside of the glass windows and said, "What a view! Incredible! Congratulations! You did a fantastic job!"

Billy was the last person to congratulate Jackson, he said, "Such a nice place! Congo!"

Jackson smiled and asked the manager, "We're sitting her for some time. Bring a few snacks and check the room arrangements for everybody!" The manager said, "Sure, Sir!" He left.

Nixie looked out of the window and noticed a big hoarding of a concert by a well-known pop sensation, popularly known as Jake Brooks. It related to music and Nixie loved music. She quickly dragged everybody's attention and said, loudly, "Guys, there is a concert here by Jake Brooks!"

Sam said, "Jake Brooks! I'm such a big fan of his!"

Nixie said, "I love music, can we please go to the concert?"

Everybody exchanged looks and Sam insisted, "Ya guys, now please don't be a spoil sport!"

Jackson looked confused and politely said, "Hmmmm, we can go!"

Billy laughed. "Oh come on people! It's Jake Brooks! Tickets would have gotten sold out on day one! How do you think you can get tickets?"

Nixie and Sam looked upset. Louis was normal and so was William. Jackson smiled, showed confidence and said, "Leave that to me, I'll arrange for VIP passes, we can definitely go. We can leave after lunch by four and return before ten so we can inaugurate the hotel, we might have to leave the concert midway"

Sam literally jumped on Jackson and said, "That's okay! Love you dad, you're the best!"

Nixie said, "Thank you very much!"

Jackson said, "That's alright! I have to leave, guys! I will check with the arrangements so you can be burden free. Relax in your room! See you all at lunch! Bye!" Everybody said bye and Jackson left.

Louis and William exchanged looks. William didn't look too happy about the concert idea! Billy noticed their reactions and said loudly to Nixie, "I don't think William will be accompanying us, I mean, he hates concerts!"

She was shocked and didn't believe it. She asked William, "Is it true?"

William answered in a low voice, "A little bit!"

Nixie smiled and said, "It's okay! I'm sure, after this concert, you will be loving concerts!" William crossed his fingers. Through the time, Louis was busy eating and just listening!

William and Nixie looked sweetly at each other. Sam hooted looking at them, "Oooooooo!" Louis and Sam high-fived and Billy did not pay attention. Nixie looked at Sam. William ruffled his hair and Sam teased them both. Nixie tried stopping him, but he didn't. He ran and Nixie ran after him. William and Louis looked at each other and took their rooms keys from the manager and left to their rooms, Billy looked around, nobody was their so even he took his room keys and left.

Later, Nixie and Sam came. They were tired and looked around. Nixie asked, "Where did everybody go?"

Sam said, "I guess they left!"

Nixie said, "So let's go!"

Both of them picked up their room keys and Sam asked the manager, "Where is dad?"

He replied, "He asked you to be in the room, he'll be there in some time," Sam nodded and they left.

Everybody was relaxing in their rooms. Louis, Sam and Billy had a good siesta. William was busy with his work on the laptop. Jackson was busy managing the inauguration and

Nixie was watching TV. Time passed by, everybody had lunch together.

Then, they were back to their rooms. Later, after a few hours, everybody dressed well for the concert and the inauguration. Everyone gathered in the lobby, except for William. They waited for William for about 10 minutes, but he did not show up, Billy said, "I told you so! We know that William hates concerts. I hope you know now, Nixie!"

Nixie was getting a bit grumpy and said, "Shut up, Billy! I'll go check. There must be a reason!" Billy was embarrassed and Nixie left.

Nixie knocked on the door. It was already open. Nixie peeped in and William stood on the balcony. Nixie walked to him and said, "Hey William! Why are you still here?" William did not respond. Nixie went to him and turned him around. She didn't get things when she saw William with tears in her eyes although William tried his best to hide his emotions. Nixie said, "Hey, why are you in tears?"

William tried hiding and said, "No, I'm not in tears. It's just…" Nixie understood that something was seriously wrong. Otherwise William wouldn't behave this way.

Nixie said, "Don't lie to me! Please tell me!"

William rubbed his face like past memories overruled his head and said "'Actually, the very first time I saw a concert, I was five and I was along with dad!"

Nixie interrupted. "That's a good thing!"

William said, "While we were returning from the concert, it was late and I was singing and jumping on the seat. I did not tie the seat belt, I wasn't even listening to dad, he opened his seatbelt to reach me while driving and tied mine. But, dad did not realize it and our car hit the tree! I was hurt but yet safe, but it was the most unfortunate incident in my life, my dad passed away!"

Nixie was speechless and felt guilty! William said, "Since then, I stopped being to concerts! They only remind of the past and I just can't take it!"

Nixie had tears in her eyes. She was embarrassed. She wasn't able to face William. Nixie said, "Very sad to know. I'm sorry, I had no idea about this. I'll tell everybody that we aren't going to concert anymore."

Nixie turned around and William stopped her and said, "But it's not a rule that all concerts are meant to be the same for me! I want to try this time!"

Nixie looked worried and said, "But I don't want you to try!"

William smiled and said, "I like you when you are worried about me!"

Nixie didn't understand that he was flirting with her. She was worried. "What kind of a person are you, you like looking at people when they are worried?"

William said, "Forget all this, we are late!"

Nixie was concerned and asked, "Are you sure?"

William smiled and said, "More than I ever was!" Nixie wasn't sure but William dragged her out of the room, locked the room and tickled Nixie to make her laugh, tickling Nixie did work and both got down to the lobby.

Everybody was waiting for them! They were all extremely surprised to see William! They had never ever expected him to be a part of the concert! Especially Billy, he thought that Nixie will learn her lesson about William but Billy learned his!

William looked at everybody. Nobody spoke. William then said, "Guys, let's hurry up. We have already missed a lot!" he rushed out. After William left, everybody looked at Nixie with puzzled expressions. "How?"

Nixie smiled like she didn't know. She did not do anything. She tried an innocent escape and said, "Let's leave people!" She left. They all exchanged looks and moved out. Sam looked very excited. It was the very first time he was attending a concert with William!

Chapter 8

Confessed the Truth that Bought Changes Along

It was late at night and Nixie, William, Jackson, Sam, Louis and Billy reached the concert venue. They stepped out of the car. A man was waiting for them. Jackson and Sam knew him and hugged him. The man took them straight into the hall through a VIP entrance. They were all excited! When they reached and settled, that man went backstage. There was nobody on stage by then but the stage and complete set up looked huge and very impressive.

Nixie casually asked, “Why isn’t Jake on stage yet?”

Billy nastily said, “Let me think. Oh I know! Because we missed a lot of concert, all thanks to William. Now we’re able to watch at least some!”

Nixie answered in exactly the same way. Billy said, “Can’t you just shut up?”

Billy then tried fixing his talk. “I was just…”

Nixie interrupted and said, “We don’t want expert comments, seriously!”

William chopped the talk and said, “It’s okay people and I’m so sorry guys!”

Nixie softly said, “It’s alright even if we’ve missed half the concert!”

Immediately, the fans started yelling and screaming. They were a rowdy lot! They were going insane because Jake was walking on stage! He said, "Hey everybody!" People went crazier when he started speaking. He said, "Are you ready for some fun?" All the fans screamed and he began singing. Everybody was dancing, including Nixie.

After an hour or so, Jake sat down on a stool and everybody was waiting for what he was going to do next. Jake was sweating but charming and said, "Okay guys, I have something new. This will be the last song for tonight; I hope you guys had fun. What we're going to do is, Micky, my technician is going to flash the spotlight on all of you. On whoever it stops, I'm going to call that person on stage. I will do exactly what that person wants! So technically I'm giving you a chance to come up here and make a wish!" Everybody yelled. Micky flashed the spotlight on the audience. Nixie wished it would stop on her because she really wanted to sing.

And Nixie whispered in William's ears, "I wish to be that person!"

William looked confused and said, "This wish is a bit too difficult." Nixie secretly used her magical power and the spotlight stopped on her. They were all surprised, especially William! Nixie looked innocent!

Then, Jake energetically announced, "We have a beautiful girl with us!"

William was a bit jealous! Then, a couple of staff members came to Nixie and took her on stage through the backstage entrance. It was full of crew members, technicians and technical devices. It looked chaotic but clean.

Nixie got on stage and Jake was blown away looking at Nixie. He came closer and William got jealous. Jake said, "Hey hi, you look great! What's your name?"

Nixie casually said, "I'm Nixie, and I'm such a big fan of music!"

When Nixie said that she was a big fan, Jake was expecting his name but she didn't say his name. Jake was impressed looking at how innocently she said that and just laughed. Nixie said, "And you're great too!"

Jake laughed and said, "Thanks, this means a lot, you're different!"

Nixie innocently asked, "Why does everyone keep saying that?" Jake smiled! He wasn't able to believe that anybody could be so beautifully innocent, he was getting attracted to her!

Jake then asked, "So, what is your wish?"

Nixie quickly said, as if she knew what she really wanted, "I want to sing with you, but on the song that I wrote! I'm so fond of singing!"

Jake thought for a few seconds and said, "Girl, your wish is complicated!"

Nixie said, "But that's all I want and nothing else!" Nixie was really stubborn and Jake wasn't able to help it because he was the one who asked her to wish!

Jake said, "People, we're going backstage! We will discuss a bit on the song and we'll be right back with something great!" Jake smartly but casually dragged Nixie backstage.

Jake then asked, "So what are we going to sing?"

Nixie said, "I have lyrics!"

Jake smiled and said, "Songs aren't that easy to make, I'd suggest to sing one of my song!"

Nixie answered, "Maybe you can sing these lyrics to the sound track of any of your songs! I really want to express how I feel! It's been so long I haven't sung!"

Jake though for a while and looked at his manager. Nixie's talk was convincing, Nixie magically got the book of lyrics in her bag. The book consisted of many lyrics. She showed it to Jake. Jake was surprised and said, "You wrote so many songs!"

Nixie smiled and innocently confessed the truth. "Well, it automatically comes, my complete journey to the human world!"

Jake didn't get her. He was amazed. His expressions turned curious and he said, "What?"

Nixie's struggle began with fixing her true, weird and innocent talk. She said, "I mean, I write about everything! Like really everything!" Jake was impressed. Nixie smiled and Jake began reading the lyrics, the lyrics defined Nixie's situation!

Jake thought Nixie was a really romantic person and said, "But that's just how you feel, what about me!"

Nixie smiled and casually said, "Well, I can't write about how you feel, so you can sing what you like!" Nixie was as genuine as she was with William. For her, it made no difference.

Jake flirtatiously said, "Well, what I feel will be so true! Let's practice!" Nixie couldn't understand that he was being flirtatious. They walked to the rehearsal room and Jake's back up musicians played for them. On stage, the instrumentals were going on and the fans weren't bored at all. They practiced for a while. By then, the backup artists occupied the stage after the instrumentals were done. James wouldn't do so much for anybody but it was Nixie! Jake was purely attracted towards her and Nixie truly wished to sing! This delay quite surprised fans but most people though Jake is just sticking to his promise! Billy was busy teasing William by singing, "Love is in danger! Love is in danger!"

William, Jackson, Sam and Louis were all so fed up of his behavior and said, together, "Shut up!" Billy became quiet then. Nixie and Jake high-fived each other in the room backstage. The crew members were admiring Nixie's potential. They glanced at Jake and had some quiet conversation only with their facial expressions among themselves. They realized that Nixie was a really potential singer! Well, of course she was! She was a mermaid after all! The lights turned off on stage and it was completely dark. It was very quiet at first. Then, the sound of footsteps was heard. The footsteps sounded like music. Soon, fireworks lit up the stage and spotlights were beamed on Nixie. She looked like a confident pop sensation. She sang:

"Since the time I am here,

I'm looking for you!

Baby where you hiding,"

Nixie's feelings were clear from this. She meant that the lover was why she came to the human world. Jake walked onto stage next. He seemed extremely flirtatious. He sang:

"Baby I'm not hiding,

I'm right before you…

You just got to realize that now!"

Jake's intention was very obvious. Nixie didn't bother about it. Her only concern was William. She was eager to notice his expression. Unknowingly, she was concerned with William. But, it was difficult for her to zoom on William's face as thousands of people distracted her and she could barely see William. Nixie sang:

"How do I realize when you saying nothing,

You got to come and tell me what's in your heart…

What you feel about me?"

Nixie sang for William but was corresponding to Jake. It was very complicated. Nixie considered Jake's words as William's feelings. Jake was energetic and blushing, he sang:

"I feel about you like I never felt before!

Baby I want to be around you,

All the time and my heart's beating for you,

Baby I love you!"

The moment he said, "I love you", William was shocked but Nixie didn't care because she thought it was just a song! Jake was being genuine about his feelings! He sang:

"I can't stop admiring,

Your smiles overwhelming,

Baby when you're around it's festive to me!

So plz come on and complete this empty place in my life,

You're the only one I want,

And I'm going to give you everything you deserve.

Do you feel just the way I do?"

Nixie was confused, she was assuming that it was William in Jake's place and she was honest to her feelings!

"How I feel…

Is maybe not really what I mean!

It's inside me,

How do I tell you what's going on,

You got to understand that on your own!

And it's time to say,

You and I can be together,

But not forever!

And definitely not like this!

Ohhh…yea…

'Cause I got a different world,

And you got a different world…

You got your own way,

And I got minc…

I've come for a reason!

And maybe it's time to say,

You and I can be together

But not forever

And definitely not like this!

You and I can't be together!"

Nixie's past was overwhelming her through the song. She had wet eyes. She was so confused and she thought that maybe human love didn't last forever. She was depressed by her own thoughts! She realized that she couldn't live with a human. All this was not going to last forever and happiness was not going to be! William didn't understand, but he thought that maybe it's just a song which was meant to be unreal. Jake misunderstood what Nixie said. As she must have thought that she was not popular and got a normal life whereas he has got an affluent lifestyle! The fact was that Nixie really had two different worlds! The one that she lived in and who she really was in was the water world. The world that she was living in for a task was the human world! Jake wanted to be positive and he said singing when Nixie was silent:

"You and I can be together,

Plz don't lose that hope inside!"

Nixie was broken on the inside, but she sang in a very high pitch!

"Tell me why?"

Jake dramatically began explaining!

"Because we're going to fight the battle till the end!

You just got to close your eye,

And trust me for a little while,

And you'll see,

Everything around is going right,

Things aren't that tough,

Like they seem to be,

And then,

You and I can be together forever

And definitely like this!"

Nixie somehow gained confidence. Then, she smiled and looked at William and then looked at Jake and said singing:

"I'm feeling good,

Don't know if it's right,

But I want to believe in you this time,

That!

You and I can be together forever

And definitely like this!

Together!"

And then Jake ended the song singing:

"Forever"

Nixie and Jake sang together and after they sang the song, they looked extremely happy. They then casually hugged each other and looking at them being so close, William was burning like fire and glowering. But Billy was having real fun! Nixie said bye to Jake and said thanks to everybody there and came down to William and the rest of the group.

Jackson appreciated Nixie and said, "You sing like a pop star!"

Billy said to impress her. "Very well done!"

Sam jumped and hugged her saying, "Awesome!" Louis exclaimed, "Man, you're incredible!"

Nixie said, "Thank you guys!" Nixie had set her eyes on William and was desperately waiting for his views on her singing. But all her hopes went down when William said, nothing at all.

Nixie wanted to ask William about his weird behavior but before she did, Jake started speaking. "Oh okay guys! I want to say, Nixie I'm a fan of yours from now on. You are an incredible artist, you made a great memory!" Nixie smiled and everybody around stared at her. Jake said, "Guys, goodnight and thank you! Thanks for being here!" He left. His fans were screaming and gradually everybody started leaving.

Nixie was expecting to hear from William and finally asked out of desperation, "How did I sing?"

William answered in a raw voice, "It was good!" He walked on.

Nixie murmured, "That's all!" Nixie ran after William and asked him to stop, Jackson, Sam, Louis and Billy had no idea that they both had stopped.

Nixie asked William, "Why are you behaving like strangers? That was just a song and don't be so jealous, you have very special place, you're a friend!"

William smiled and hugged her and said, "You looked stunning and sang a fabulous song!" Nixie was finally happy! William's words meant more than anything else could.

They were on their way to the car but a few crew members of Jake's team were running and yelling out Nixie's name. Nixie and William stopped.

Jake's crew member asked Nixie, "Jake wants to meet you, can you please come?"

Nixie was stunned and was thinking about what she should do. But before she answered, William said, "We're getting late, come on Nixie let's go!"

Another member said, "Please it's just a matter of a few minutes!"

Nixie thought that it was just a matter of a few minutes, so she decided to go and therefore said, "Let's go! I mean it's just a matter of few minutes, come on William!"

William was helpless and followed Nixie. Everyone left. Jackson, Sam, Louis and Billy had no idea where Nixie and William were. They were all trying to call them, but their contact was not reachable. Jackson was worried about getting late! But they couldn't even leave.

Nixie and William reached Jake's green room with his staff. They opened the door for both of them and left immediately. Nixie and William walked in, and Jake was lying on the couch, reading a magazine. As Nixie and William walked in, Jake stood up. He looked excited. "Hey! Hi!" Nixie and Jake hugged.

Nixie said, "Hi, good to see you again!"

William said, in a very low volume. "Hi!"

Jake said, "Sit down, please!"

Nixie smiled and said sure. They sat down, as did Jake.

Jake said, "You are too talented and extremely gorgeous, I'm completely blown away!"

Nixie was happy and said, "Thank you very much! You are an incredible artist! I mean you picked up everything so quick although it was almost like making a new song!"

Jake smiled. He blushed a bit. "Thanks, I wondered if you would want to record a duet with me!" Nixie looked at William, and William's expression was as though he was saying "I told so!"

Nixie thought, "Stuck again! What do I do?" Nixie was uncomfortable. "Well, actually…"

Jake realized she felt awkward and said, "It's okay! If you aren't ready now," he said, giving her his contact, "Just give me a call whenever you need me!"

Nixie smiled and accepted his contact and said, "Thanks a ton!"

They were awkwardly quiet for a few seconds. But then, Jake asked curiously, "Well, who is he?"

Nixie was going to introduce him, but William introduced himself. "Hi, I'm William Thomas!"

Jake said, "Hey are you the son of Drake Thomas, the well-known businessman?" William smiled and nodded. Jake smiled and said, "Nice to meet you!" Nixie knew nothing about how rich William was and that he was royalty.

Jake then asked, "Do you guys want to have something?" They said, no. Jake then asked, "William, are you are Nixie's friend?" Jake was into Nixie. He wanted to know if she was in a relationship or not. William smiled and said, "Boyfriend." Jake and Nixie both had the same reaction stunned reaction.

"What?" said Nixie.

William said, "Yes. You heard right. We have to go now. It was great meeting you! See ya!" Jake stopped him and said, "Relax, give me your contact!"

William gave his contact and again wanted to rush. Jake stopped him again and said, "Nixie's contact!"

William took Jake's phone and said, "I'll type it for you." He typed it. Nixie wanted to say something, but William literally dragged her out. Jake understood that William was insecure. William and Nixie said bye and left. Jake read the contact and chased William. He came out of his room and stopped him. William told Nixie to wait and he alone walked towards Jake. Jake smiled and said, "You love her, right?"

William was shocked and then laughed. He said, "How do know that? I mean I'm her boyfriend but"

Jake laughed and said, "There is a digit-less in this contact!" They laughed and William was shy about his act.

Jake said, "She's very special, don't let her go!"

William and Jake shake hands. William said, "Thanks dude, thanks a lot! Sorry to treat you wrongly, you're amazing!"

Nixie was waiting for William. She said, "What's going on between you two? Do either of you care that I'm still here?" Nixie had a strong feeling that something secretive and confidential was going on between both. She was curious to know what exactly they had talked about.

Jake tapped William and said "Go!" They waved goodbye and Nixie and William left.

Jake was going to his room when his manager said, "I got you the pictures you asked for!" His manager got a call and left. Jake looked at the pictures and it was him with Nixie on stage!

Jake murmured, "I have a pretty big crush on you girl, you're amazing!"

Jake had feelings for Nixie, but he did understand that William and Nixie had an incredible bond. Jake then relaxed in his room and Nixie and William were rushing out.

Jackson, Sam, Louis and Billy were still waiting for them.

Jackson, Sam, Louis and Billy watched Nixie and William coming. Jackson said, "Where have you guys been?"

Before they could say anything in response to it, Jackson said, "Oh! Just forget all that! We will talk about it later. Get in the car, we're already late!" They all sat in the car and left.

When they settled down in the car, and relaxed, they talked about the reason why Nixie and William were late. Jackson asked William, "Tell us what happened!"

Nixie and William looked at each other and they began laughing!

William said, "Don't ask, that's a long story!"

Sam asked in excitement, "Tell it in short! Come on!"

Nixie started with what happened. "Well, actually, Jake wanted to meet me regarding the singing thing so we met him!"

Sam said, "Guys, have you both met Jake?" William and Nixie nodded. Sam screamed and said, "Oh my God!"

Nixie and William told them everything that happened. Everybody was listening curiously. Billy was disappointed. He expected a fight between William and Nixie but it never happened. Billy was listening carefully and silently, but yet behaved as if he wasn't concerned at all.

They were stuck in traffic and Jackson did not mention it, but he was worried. Nixie understood. So did everybody else, but everyone was helpless, except for Nixie. She closed her eyes for a few seconds and it did not seem abnormal. She used magic. In a minute, traffic began to move. It seemed like a miracle in New York. Soon, the heavy traffic areas were like highways!

Jackson was extremely happy and thanked God. The moment Jackson joined his hands and thanked God, Nixie felt good. She felt like someone had respected her help. Maybe unknowingly, but he did respect it after all. She was overwhelmed and she started liking the human world!

They were soon in the hotel. The hotel was shining gloriously and was decorated with lights and flowers. It looked beautiful. No one could get their eyes off the hotel! Jackson and Sam were proud and touched. The media and the guests were already in the hotel. As Jackson's car reached the main door, fireworks brightened the black sky! They had a warm welcome with music and were asked to get onto the red carpet! The media was ready with questions. People greeted and congratulated each other. They walked into the hotel. The seating arrangements were ready in the lobby. Most guests had already arrived!

William, Nixie, Sam, Louis and Billy sat on the front area in round tables. Jackson stood up on stage. The stage was built under a beautiful chandelier with big diamond-like stones. The press was desperate to hear from Jackson. Jackson seemed confident and well-groomed.

He started his speech that said, "Thank you everybody for being here. This function is extremely prestigious for me and my son and my wife who is close to God. I'm sure she'd be proud today because building this hotel on this place was her dream, when I started my career. It hasn't been many years since. This hotel is prestigious for me because of my wife. I'm proud to announce that our hotel was a five-star hotel from the beginning! This is the proudest moment for me and my son. I want to mention a couple of my friends who have been around me and I'm thankful to them for having given me something that one can't buy: love and a feeling of being home! Thank you, William, for everything, and of course,

Louis, Nixie and Billy! You guys are great! My son is the most understanding person in the world! I wish for nothing else. God bless everybody! I hope you have a great time. Thanks a lot!"

Everybody cheered and clapped for him. Sam was happy, but missed his mom. He hid his emotions. Jackson understood and hugged him tight, trying his best to be his mom, but it didn't work!

After everybody congratulated Jackson, they began dancing. Everybody was dragged to the dance floor. Initially, they played loud music where people got insane. For Nixie, clubbing was an all-new experience. Nixie preferred isolating herself. She seemed like she was not a big fan of such dance moves! William, Jackson, Sam, Louis, Billy and everybody else was busy dancing. Nixie chose a corner and sat down. She thought something wild was going on, on the dance floor and she wasn't interested in it. William looked around and didn't find Nixie on the dance floor. He panicked but saw Nixie drinking juice. He went to her.

William realized that maybe Nixie wasn't fond of dance. But, he knew that she loved music. William dragged Jackson out of the dance floor. He whispered in his ears, "Can we play something else, maybe like ball dancing music?"

Jackson couldn't understand why and asked, "But why?" William ruffled his hair. He then pointed at Nixie. He was blushing and expecting some help from Jackson.

Jackson tapped William on his shoulder. He said, "Your job is done! No worries!" Jackson left to the manager. William stopped him again and whispered in his ears. It seemed confidential. William had a different spark in his eyes. Jackson walked out with a smile. He picked up Sam from the dance floor. Sam asked him why he was doing that. Jackson kept his forefinger on his lips and avoided Sam's question. Jackson and Sam walked out to the garden with the manager. They were discussing something important. Sam was jumping and dancing. He was amazed at something and the manager was just nodding!

Meanwhile William sat beside Nixie and asked her, "Hey! Are you fine?"

Nixie casually said, "I'm not a big fan of disco dance and I'm feeling low!"

William thought, "I was so right about her feelings!" William looked happier than before. Nixie misunderstood that he was happy about Nixie's unease, although she did not mention it.

William was getting desperate with time. It was very obvious, because he was bouncing his leg up and down, and tapping his fingers on one another. Nixie was shaken, but avoided saying anything.

Nixie and William sat quietly next to each other. William looked around restlessly. Jackson lifted his thumb as a sign that something was done. William's excitement was at its peak.

The music changed to light ballroom dance music. Nixie was surprised. Everybody on the dance floor danced as couples. Jackson and Sam danced together. Louis and Billy found their partners. William stood up and went on one knee and extended his hand and said, "May I take this opportunity to ask you to dance with me?" Nixie was thrilled and overwhelmed. She smiled and said, "I would love to dance with you!"

Nixie kept her palm on William's palm, accepting his proposal. Nixie stood up and they danced. They were close to each other and had the least concern about the rest of the world. Nixie said, while dancing, "This is my first dance with somebody! You may have danced before?"

William smiled looking at the ground. He looked into Nixie's eyes and said, "This is my first dance with the most beautiful girl on this planet!" Nixie was blown away and amazed. She couldn't believe her ears. She was definitely happy!

William was staring at Nixie all the time. Nixie was casual in the beginning but soon, she became shy for no reason. She wasn't even able to explain the feeling she was going through to herself. The place went dark with a few red lights. Nixie felt uncomfortable dancing when it grew dark. She thought of leaving. William held her hand and stopped her. Immediately, the place went completely dark. There was just a spotlight on Nixie and William. Nixie had surprises over surprises. She couldn't react much to the situation. She tried to figure out what was going on. She politely asked, "What's going on?"

William bought her closer and said, "Isn't it romantic?" William then went down on one knee. Nixie had the same expression. Jackson was extremely happy for William. Sam was enthusiastic. Louis hoped that everything happens well because he knew very well that Nixie was not like other girls she was very difficult to impress and it was very difficult to grab her attention! Everybody formed a circle around them. Although it was really romantic, William was desperate. His heart was beating faster. He was nervous, because he really loved Nixie!

He said, "I don't know how you feel about me, Nixie, but I want to let you know how I feel about you! You are an incredible person. You are the most beautiful person on this planet. Not just on the outside, but also within! You are the only person for whom my heart skips a beat every time I look at you. I love you Nixie, will you marry me?"

Nixie had mixed emotions. She loved it, but was confused. She was trying to figure out how she felt about William. Thoughts and memories of the time they spent together were going on in Nixie's head. She was a real and genuine person who never believed in making fake and false promises or commitments. She assured herself that she was in love with William. He was scared that he may be rejected, but he wasn't upset at the thought of rejection. He was definitely upset by the thought that he may lose Nixie forever!

Nixie smiled and blushed. She walked close to William and said, "Thank you very much for making me realize how I feel about you. I love you too, William, I really do!"

William's heart skipped a beat. He was extremely happy. He jumped off the ground and lifted Nixie, turned her around and said, "I was waiting for this day for long! I love you! I love you so much!"

Nixie was equally happy and said, "I love you too, love you so much!"

Everybody around cheered them on. The lights turned on. Jackson, Sam and Louis hugged both of them. They were all happy! Nixie and William hugged each other and danced till 3:00 AM!

Chapter 9

Couldn't Win after Losing

Everybody had a great time. Later, William dropped Nixie in her room. Before she shut the door, they looked at each other. Nixie was blushing. They hugged each other. Then, William left and Nixie shut the door. Both said, nothing but had a really sweet and thoughtful unspoken conversation. Words meant nothing! William ruffled his hair and went into his room which was right below Nixie's room. They were lost in each other and couldn't think of anything else! Nixie almost forgot who she was and behaved like a human!

After Nixie shut the door, she threw her purse on the bed and held the wall as she removed her shoe. She said, "I am in love! Oh my God, I just can't believe it, I didn't even realize that all this time, I was in love with William! It really is the most beautiful feeling ever!" She lay down on the bed, smiling and blushing, and thinking of William and nothing else. She almost forgot about the mission which was why she was in the human world as a human being! Nixie closed her eyes as a recap of all the memories with William was going on in her head.

Nixie suddenly thought of Yara! She stood up straight and was stressed. She had sweat on her forehead that almost dropped down on the floor. Her head was spinning and it was nothing less than a nightmare! Soon, she was sweating profusely. Nixie was confused and her eyes were red, as if she had committed a crime and didn't know now how to set it right. Nixie began crying and hid her face with both her hands. Her head was held down. The pressure on nerves was clearly seen on her forehead as her nerves swelled.

She cried soundlessly. She was shattered. Her face turned completely red! Then, Nixie said, in a low but intense voice, "Sakhi!"

Nixie looked extremely helpless and she was torn apart.

On the other side, William was so happy that he couldn't sleep. He was lying on the bed and thinking of Nixie all the time. He was thinking, smiling and blushing. William couldn't believe his destiny that everything so great happened to him in such a short period of time! An unexpected girl had come into his life and they fell in love! William lay on the bed. He had already turned off the lights, but a yellow color bulb was bright under a beautiful lantern. The lantern wasn't the kind of lantern that existed in the olden times. It was creatively beautiful and William was continuously looking at it, and thinking about Nixie! William politely said, "Nixie is truly my true love!" Then, he closed his eyes and fell asleep.

Nixie's room was messy. She was sitting down on the floor in a corner. She was talking to herself. She said, "William is my true love. This means that my mission accomplished! But I love him, I really do, everyone was absolutely right! It's going to be extremely difficult! Please help me God! Please!"

Nixie was broken within. She could just see darkness ahead of her and nothing else. She didn't know how she was going to handle herself. She had no idea how to handle her emotions and how she was going to tell William. She wasn't even in a situation where she could reveal the truth! She knew she'd be broken and William would stop trusting anybody. Nixie knew what she was doing. It was incorrect and ridiculously mean, but she wasn't able to make a decision and was completely lost. She needed help desperately, but when she looked around, nobody was around to help her. She was weeping nonstop and murmured, "Why is this human world so difficult? What will I tell William? I am so lost! He is going to hate me. He must hate me! Otherwise, he will be broken and I can't see him in pain! Please hate me, William! Hate me! All that I did was for my friend, but I love you, I'm not a fake!"

Nixie understood well that she had to make William hate her. Otherwise, William would be torn apart. Nixie never wanted that to happen! Nixie cried so hard that her eyes turned red and she was barely able to open them wide! She wasn't even able to see things clearly because her brain was tired. Nixie had lived the life of a mermaid and had never faced such difficult situations that humans do. She had never faced so much confusion and such complication. It was nerve-wracking for her! She was so tired and she fell asleep unknowingly!

It was 5:00 AM. Nixie gradually woke up and then rubbed her eyes to see things clearly. When she touched, she realized that her teardrops were still on her cheeks. She had to push herself to get up as she was feeling low! She failed to stand properly. She had barely slept for an hour and a half, and that was not enough for a stressed human body! She sat on the floor, with the support of the bed and then looked at the watch. She didn't know how to handle things. But, she also knew that she had to. Nixie grumbled. "Human life isn't meant for me! It never was!" she had acidic burps and she spontaneously kept her hand on her mouth to control herself. She felt uneasy and sick! She ran to the wash basin and puked. She had no idea what was happening to her, but she wasn't fine at all! She wiped her mouth and splashed water on her face. She stood for about a minute and then came to the living room. She drank water and walked to the phone. She used magic and closed her eyes for a few seconds and then picked up the phone and numbers started pressing themselves! She called a doctor outside of the hotel as she didn't wish to let anybody else know about her illness.

The doctor answered her call.

Nixie spoke softly, and said, "This is Nixie here. I need some help from you!"

The doctor thought it was really strange and said, "This is my personal contact. How did you even get this number? Come to my clinic and then I can help you!"

Nixie was too low to actually give an excuse. She used magic and the doctor was under Nixie's spell! She could use magic as she was allowed to use magic for any human need! Nixie asked, "I'm feeling terrific and getting acidic burps. I just puked, I had nothing bad, I just didn't eat last night and I'm stressed!"

The doctor had a poker face and said, "It's nothing to worry. You are stressed. Take an energy drink and some solid food and you may have a medicine for your headache, too, I will suggest one for you." The doctor wanted to continue, but Nixie seemed so low that she kept the phone down and her head was spinning. She was giddy and fell down on the bed. She used magic and arranged everything that she had to take! It concluded with juice, packed food, medicine, protein chocolates and fruits. She ate medicine and everything that appeared. She felt better but was stressed even then. Food and other stuff did help her physically but mentally she was broken!

She looked around for her phone and found it under the bed. She dragged it out and looked at it for a few seconds. She started weeping! She banged her head on the phone and forcefully sat on the couch!

It was 6:00 AM by then. Nixie was scared to initiate any step!

By then, William was awake. His alarm rang right next to his ears. He woke up at once and he smilingly looked excited. He couldn't get Nixie off his head! He looked at his phone and picked it up very gently and kissed his phone. He said, "I can do anything to make my princess smile and hear her voice!" William renamed Nixie to princess. He got off the bed and looked at his face on the mirror and said, "People look really different when they are in love, so charming!"

William wasn't admiring himself but he was definitely admiring the feeling of love! It was deeper than the ocean, wider than space, more intense than the sun, and much cooler than ice. He was happier than God. He was blessed more than anyone else. It was purer than milk, and more prestigious than a King's crown! All descriptions failed before William as his feelings for his princess, Nixie, couldn't be put into words! William smiled brightly and said, to himself, "I am the richest person on this planet, I found Nixie, and I need nothing else! Thank you God for nothing but just for Nixie! Thank you!"

William was happy like he was never before. On the other side, the absolute opposite occurred. Nixie was upset like she was never before! Nixie dressed up, not very well, but not too badly either. She didn't want to show that she was broken because she had learned by now that fake expressions were important in a fake world. She knew that people don't portray the real situation ever. She left the hotel without telling anybody and without her luggage. She stopped a taxi and sat inside. She reached the beach, got off the taxi and used magic to pay the taxi driver. She walked on the beach. There was nobody around. It was extremely quiet.

Nixie walked close to the sea and touched the waves. She had an expressionless face. Then, she started crying! Nixie had no control over her tears. They were just rolling down her cheek and she wasn't able to stop them. Nixie stood still for long. A few people came to the beach. A few went jogging, a few did yoga, a few did meditation and a few were listening to music with ear phones on and silently looking around.

Nixie was the most different being on the beach because she did nothing and was standing still. After some time, Nixie's tears dried up and she took a deep breath. She smilingly, but not happily at all, murmured to herself, "Maybe now I am strong enough to act!" She calmly closed her eyes for a few seconds and then opened them. She pretended that everything was normal like before. Nixie looked at her phone. She was mentally collecting her broken pieces and trying to fix them, at least she was pretending to do so! She dialed William's number.

William just stepped out of the washroom when his phone rang. William walked closer and took it off the plug where it was charging. He smiled and blushed, noticing that it was Nixie's call. He looked at the watch and it was 7:00 AM. He was surprised. After a few rings, William answered and said, "Hello princess, I didn't know you were so desperate!" William was flirting.

Nixie said, without reacting to William's flirtatious attitude, "Hi, I am here on the beach! I want you to come here as soon as possible, it's very urgent and important! Please don't tell anybody else!"

William avoided Nixie's blunt words and focused on the fact that she had invited him for something special and that too, alone. He politely said, "You mean alone? Oh, which beach?" Nixie did not bother about William's flirtatious attitude and said, "There is just one beach near to the hotel!"

William smiled and said, "I got it! I'll be there in less than half-an-hour!" Nixie said, "Okay, see you then, bye!" William also said, "Bye!" and both cut the call on their phones.

William was extremely happy. The back of his mind forced him to be happy after thinking of everything that had happened between Nixie and him. William was desperately expecting something good. He was dressed casually. Then, he removed something good to wear. After he had changed, he picked up his room keys and was about to leave. It was then that the intercom rang and grabbed his attention. He answered. It was Jackson on the phone. "Jackson here, why aren't you guys here for breakfast, yet? Nixie isn't even answering calls! What's up?"

William smiled and said, "She left for the beach early in the morning. I'm going too, so I hope you understand!" Jackson said, teasingly. "I totally do! I don't want to mess up the love birds!"

Both laughed and Jackson said, "Okay then! Carry on. Remember, we have to leave for Sacramento this afternoon! Don't be late!"

William answered, "Sure! I'll be on time, I mean we will be on time!"

Both smiled and William said, "See you guys at the airport then!"

Jackson said, "Sure, I'll get your luggage wrapped. We'll take it along with us to the airport, you guys can join us there!"

William nodded and said, "Okay, thanks, thanks a lot!"

Jackson casually said, "Oh come on! You take good care, bye!"

William ruffled his hair and said, "You too, bye!"

Both kept the phone down. William walked out of his room and got into the elevator. When he was passing by the lobby, Billy noticed him. He seemed extremely enthusiastic and murmured "Where the hell is this man going so early? Not even ready for breakfast yet!" Billy peeped into the breakfast buffet and noticed Jackson, Louis and Sam in there.

He thought for a moment and then murmured to himself, "I should chase William!" He also left to chase William looking for where he was heading to. He did it happily. Billy was extremely interested in spying on William. William stopped a taxi and sat in and right after Billy stopped a taxi and sat inside. He instructed the driver, pointing at William's taxi. "Chase that taxi!"

Both reached the beach. William got off the taxi and paid the taxi driver. He was so happy that he gave an extra tip to the driver saying, "Keep this too!" He walked on the beach. He looked around for Nixie and she stood quietly, at a distance, he slowly walked towards her.

In just some time, Billy reached there and murmured under his breath, "A beach? I mean, really?" He got off the taxi and began walking ahead.

The taxi driver stopped him and said, "Hey, what about my money?"

Billy then realized that he had to pay him. He looked for his wallet, which was supposed to be in his pocket. But unfortunately, it wasn't there. Billy said, "Damn it!"

He then tried convincing the taxi driver, saying, "Hey, I forgot my wallet in my hotel room! If you can wait, I'll take you back to my hotel and pay the whole amount. Is that okay with you?"

The taxi driver thought for few seconds and said, "Okay! But it's going to be a whole lot of money!"

Billy casually said, like it was nothing, "It's all fine dude!" He walked faster to the beach and looked around and noticed that William was tapping Nixie's shoulder!

Billy exclaimed in a very low voice, "Oh, so both are here!" Billy ran the fastest he could. He didn't want to miss anything. He hid at the back of a tree and was able to hear every word they said! He truly was a focused spy!

Nixie said, hi and William noticed her upset face. He couldn't make out the reason and asked her with concern, "Are you okay?"

Nixie lied in no time and hid her emotions, pretending to be fine. "Oh no, I mean nothing, I'm alright!"

William accepted her lie. He trusted Nixie. He said, "You called me here! I mean, there must be something special or important that I should know. I understand that you want to wish me luck for the racing jam, but if there is something else, you can tell me!"

William teased Nixie and flirted with her. Nixie avoided him, and regaining all her strength, she bluntly said, "I don't know if its special but it is important. Listen, I'm going back to

Finland!" The moment Nixie said, that, the atmosphere began changing. The clouds turned gray. The atmosphere changed. It was dawn for a minute, and dusk in another! It seemed like nature was indicating to Nixie that the step she had initiated would be harmful and wrong! The breezes were strong and high tides hit the ocean!

The weather girls on different channels said, "Sudden change in the atmosphere, there seems to be a likelihood of a tsunami in the future, people are instructed to not visit the beach today. The weather change happens once in hundreds of years! Be careful, be safe. We will report updates soon!" It was intense. Due to climatic changes, people began leaving the beach. Soon, Nixie and William were left on the beach and nobody else was around.

Nixie's attitude shocked William. He couldn't believe his ears. He said, "What? No jokes please!"

Nixie controlled her feelings. Being strong, she was blunt. She knew that if she lost her blunt attitude, she wouldn't be able to control her emotions. "It's no joke! I've completed my book and whatever we had between us is all over!"

William was in shock. He didn't understand anything. He thought Nixie was a nice person, but he was in a dilemma. He said "You won't even stay till my racing jam!"

Nixie was firm. She said, "No, I'm sorry!" William was not able to control his feelings and tears rolled down his cheek. He wasn't able to stop his tears. The moment his tears fell, Nixie used magic and a shell appeared out of the ground. It gradually opened and William's tear drops were collected in it. It was a magical process and nobody even noticed it.

After the tears were collected, the shell automatically disappeared. Nixie said in the same tone. "Well, I just wanted to complete my book and I did it. Thank you very much for showing me around and I assure that I will reimburse all that you had spent on me!"

Nixie purposely hurt William. She wanted him to hate her. Nixie knew that she had to go back to her world and she thought it was the best way to make William hate her and he will be able to get over her. William was hurt and was trying to understand. He saw that Nixie was hiding something, but Nixie's mask was making everything unclear. William thought this was the real side of Nixie but he wasn't able to accept it because he truly loved Nixie!

William said, "It's okay if you don't want to accept my love, but don't disrespect it! It is really true Nixie!"

Nixie had the same feelings for him, but they were suppressed. Nixie said, "Listen, I'm sorry, I'm getting late for the flight and I have to leave now. My taxi is on hold. I hope you understand, it was nice meeting you, I have to go! Bye!"

William was torn. He was completely stranded. He said, "I understand!" He turned around and left. Nixie turned the other side and began crying! She was not able to control her feelings.

Billy sarcastically stood before William and nastily said, "I guess your love story ended before it even started!" William was not embarrassed. He truly loved Nixie. But he believed in not giving ears to whatever Billy said. He was hurt and disappointed by Nixie's behavior! He left and Billy sat in the taxi that he had come by.

Nixie was in tears and said, "I am sorry! I really wish you start hating me. Please get me out of your life. I was blunt. I'm sorry, because if I would stay even a minute longer in front of you, I wouldn't have been able to fake my emotions! I won't be able to forgive myself but you please do forgive me! I'm sorry!"

While travelling back to the hotel, William cried all the way. He didn't understand the dual personality that Nixie showcased. Somewhere, his heart wasn't accepting the rude side of Nixie!

On the other side, Nixie cried bitterly on the beach. Everybody was looking at her. She wiped her tears and walked to the extreme end of the beach where there was nobody. She was walking slowly. Each step she took was accompanied with tears. She had a choked throat and wasn't even able lift her legs. She was literally dragging and pushing herself ahead. She finally reached the end. She sat in a corner and it was an extremely painful experience for Nixie!

William asked the taxi driver to stop midway. "Listen, please stop right here. Change in plans!" He got off the taxi and paid the driver.

He walked on the streets where William and Nixie had walked together. He missed Nixie. After all that happened, William wasn't able to hate her!

William walked miles thinking about Nixie and her strange behavior all the way.

Billy reached the hotel. He got off the taxi and said, "Thanks dude. Hold on for a minute!" He went to his room and brought his wallet. He paid the driver. Billy seemed happy because he wanted to see William and Nixie broken up. He never realized how intense their love was. For Billy it was always about short term relationships.

Billy turned around and Jackson walked towards him and said, "Where were you? We were waiting for you during breakfast?"

Billy pretended to be sad and said, "I have something important to tell you guys. It isn't good. Can we get in first?" Jackson nodded. He seemed worried. They walked together into the hotel.

Sometime later, William reached the hotel and went straight into his room. The staff had already wrapped his stuff. He looked around his room and somebody knocked the door. William opened the door. Jackson, Billy, Louis and Sam were there. William was surprised, seeing all of them together in his room. He asked, "Hi! All of you are here!" Sam and Louis hugged him tight and said, "We already know, stop hiding!" William burst into tears.

Everybody supported William, but nobody was able to trust such unfortunate and unexpected happenings. They were all equally shocked, including Billy, but Billy was also happy at the same time. William said, with a choked voice, "All girls are the same, even Nixie! They are all mean!"

Louis tried his best to calm William down and said, "Don't stress! You have a major racing jam! Remember, that's your real dream!"

William was fed up of his life and everything materialistic. He said, "I don't want to race!" Louis and everybody else knew that he was heartbroken. Billy was enjoying the situation but didn't show it.

Louis said, "Shut up! You can't let your dream slip from your hand; you have worked so hard for it!"

Billy found it offensive. He was a part of the race and said, "Hey, even I am going to race!"

Everybody looked at him grumpily and Jackson said, "Not now Billy!" It was a clear sign to shut up!

William then said, "Why do people do this to me!"

Nobody had an answer. They could only console him and show him concern. They walked down the lobby and were all set to leave.

William, Jackson, Louis, Sam and Billy were leaving for the airport. On the other side, Nixie sat like a statue on the beach without moving. She was expressionless and had tears! She had tears of love on her palm. She closed it tight and said, "The last lesson of the human world! Humans have everything and get anything they work for. But, they have no satisfaction. I love you, William. I really love you!" Nixie had learned enough.

Nixie was all alonc. William had people around who cared for him. But, internally he was absolutely alone. William was still thinking of Nixie after everything that had happened. William's eyes were filled with tears. He wiped his face every now and then. He walked on in the airport with everybody else. Nixie was on the beach. Everybody thought she must have left for Finland just like she said. The truth was that Nixie didn't go anywhere. But of course, she had to leave for her world, which she did not tell anyone about. She wasn't waiting for anything. She wasn't able to prepare herself to leave the human world or William! William and Nixie were pretty much in the same situation. The only difference was that Nixie lied and William didn't. Nixie's mission was about getting love tears and she did. She won the battle that she had started but had lost true love. It meant more than anything else! She couldn't completely win after losing!

Chapter 10

A Life-Changing Decision

William was inside the plane and sat in the window seat. William was in tears. Jackson was worried for him. Louis was concerned about him. Billy thought William was overreacting, because for Billy, it was like new girl each day. He didn't care much. Sam couldn't agree that Nixie would turn out to be such a devil! He was confused. Sam thought it wasn't right to talk about the past.

Louis just wasn't able to see William in so much pain. He was also sitting next to him, so he tapped William's shoulder and hugged him and said, "Please, don't cry buddy, control yourself!"

William was broken. His throat was choked. He definitely needed a tight hug. When he settled a bit, he said, "How can Nixie do this to me? After all that we had between us, I don't understand! I really love her. I still can't hate her! I don't believe she is the same person. I won't be able to love again, Louis, never! Please ask her to come back in my life, please, I beg!"

Louis was helpless and speechless at the same time. He didn't know what to say and everybody was in tears except for Billy. Billy took it easy.

William said, "It's impossible to live without her! I love her!" It was then that Billy thought that it was something serious. He was touched. Billy realized that maybe William was really in love with Nixie and it wasn't just an attraction. But, he was not so sure yet!

William found out Nixie's face in the clouds. He was missing her because he knew that she was not going to be back. William smiled like he had found Nixie on the clouds, waiting for him. William said, "Nixie!"

Nixie was still on the beach. Her hair was messed up. Tears flowed down her eyes. She had no other expression on her face. The worst part was that she couldn't even regret it, because it was her choice.

Time passed and Nixie didn't realize that she had to leave. She slept on the beach that night. She wasn't concerned that something wrong may happen. She was concerned with nothing at all!

The next afternoon, William stood near his racing car. He was already on the tracks and so was Billy. Billy looked happier than ever. Louis was the Head of the Car Mechanic team, so he was busy instructing his team. Every time he looked at William, he could feel his pain! Jackson and Sam sat with the crowd that had come to watch the race. They were praying for William and hoped for the best.

Meanwhile, a volleyball hit Nixie on her head. She suddenly woke up. She had slept for very long!

"Ouch!" she said, when she woke up. She smiled and thought, "It must be Sam!"

Just then, a little boy about five walked close to her and said, "I'm sorry, we didn't know you were here!"

Nixie returned the ball and said, "It's alright!" The boy left happily. Nixie realized by then that she was day dreaming. She wasn't crying anymore, but was trying her best to regain her strength, so that she could leave. She looked around and sun was at its peak. She noticed a big rock further ahead. She looked at it for a while and then stood up. Nixie walked towards the rock.

There were lots of people around, but nothing bothered her. She walked on without looking around. A few people around her who noticed her thought that it was rather awkward that she did this, but nobody asked her anything. They could not ask, either, because Nixie wouldn't have wanted them to. She used magic on people on the beach so nobody could ask her although people who noticed her got really curious!

William was prepared for the race, but not mentally. He didn't want to be a part of the race anymore. But surely, he had pressure on his head, which was why he decided to race. The screaming fans, media, publicity, beautiful cheerleaders cheering the racers, fans wearing t-shirts with William's name - what else would anybody need? But it was not what William wanted. He needed and wished just to have Nixie around, even if it meant that all this would go away. William looked around and was trying to understand why people liked him. He thought that people may like and appreciate his art and his work world over, but nobody loved his core. He missed Nixie, which was why all the negative thoughts blocked his mind. He was obsessed with Nixie. There was tremendous noise, but for William, since he lived somewhere lost in thought and in the memories of Nixie, there was silence!

In the meantime, Nixie used magic and lifted her hand high up to the rock. She closed her eyes as she created an invisible wall around the big rock. She looked like a dead person. She walked inside the wall. Because of the magic, nobody was able to see her or what she was doing. She had disappeared for everybody around her. She stood up on the rock and looked at the water.

Nixie was ready to leave and William was ready to race. They were each heading for something extremely important. Both of them wanted each other and loved each other, but were not together. Their tears had dried but the pain increased!

William began the race and Nixie walked closer to the edge of the rock. William drove on, but he was not alert at all. He was on the first in the beginning and almost forgot that he was racing. Nixie was overruling him and he was stuck in the past. He wasn't accepting the situation or maybe he didn't want to! He banged the steering wheel of the car and lost control over the car and the car hit the wall. The last word William said, was "Nixie!"

William had unfortunately met with an accident. Everyone was shocked. It was a wreck that brought everybody down to silence. For a few seconds, people were stunned and absolutely blank.

The moment William had said, Nixie, Nixie said "William!" and then jumped into the ocean. It wasn't an ordinary jump! She went like a rocket and immediately turned into a mermaid!

William had an accident whereas Nixie turned into her real self, a mermaid, and went in her real world, the water world!

William was unconscious. His car literally was on fire. Soon, the fire was put out and an ambulance reached. The race was over and everybody was with William. Sam was crying and Jackson was scared that after such a major accident, William may die, Louis was about to faint. Billy was ashamed of himself. For the first time ever, he was worried and upset for William. William was placed in the ambulance and media covered the incident. Jackson, Sam, Louis, and Billy followed the ambulance.

On the other side, William's mother was unaware of all this. She was with her doctor; she seemed to be happy and thought to herself, "Very strange that nobody called to tell me about the race!" She picked up her phone and called Louis, he did not reply.

Louis was tensed and didn't know how to face William's mother. He knew that she was a heart patient and such news could be dangerous for her health. Catherine tried Jackson's contact. Jackson and Louis sat together and exchanged looks. Jackson avoided the call. They knew they couldn't do it for long, but at that moment, they were speechless. Catherine was worried because nobody answered her call.

Nixie was travelling downwards, further and further into the depths of the ocean! Nixie then reached her world and all the mermaids gathered around her, Nixie looked at them. Everybody thought it was a true miracle that Nixie had performed.

They had hope in their eyes and Nixie magically bought love tears and showed them all. All the mermaids, one by one, hugged Nixie. They had nothing to convey and were just happy with no other thought on their minds. Nixie then walked towards Yara and touched her. Nixie's hands were shaking and tears fell from her eyes, and each turned into pearl. Nixie opened the shell and dropped love tears on Yara's eyes. Everybody was patiently waiting for Yara to get back to life. They believed that everything will be fine.

At the same time, on land, William was taken to hospital and was admitted in the ICU. William's position was really bad.

Everybody's entry was prohibited. Doctors were busy with William's treatment. Although it was complicated, they were trying their best. Catherine was repeatedly calling Louis. There was no way of hiding, so he had to pick up the call.

Catherine was tensed and said, "Something wrong, son? Why weren't you answering my calls?" Louis looked at Jackson and his head was bent down. Louis gathered his wits and replied, "Aunty! We are sorry. Unfortunately, William met with a car accident during the race!" Catherine was shocked and felt pressure on her heart. She wasn't able to breathe properly. Memories of William's dad's past flew into Catherine's mind.

She remembered how William's dad had died in a car accident and how broken William was. She yelled out of pressure on the heart and dropped the phone. Louis reacted intensely, saying "Aunty!" Louis was nervous and Catherine was alone in the room, lying on the ground.

Louis looked at everybody and said, "We have to rush. Jackson Aunty isn't fine!"

Jackson immediately said, "Let's go!" Louis and Jackson had left for the hotel. They were extremely nervous. Billy and Sam stayed back in the hospital to check on William's condition. Sam was scared and Billy moved towards Sam and consoled him, Billy had built an emotional relation for the first time ever.

There were emotional changes in everybody. Billy wasn't a bad person anymore, but was lost in the glamour of the world. He had finally found himself and realized that there was much more to life than he thought. He was upset for somebody he disliked before. Billy discovered his new self during all this time. The love between two people could be so strong. That made Billy re-think his judgments and calculations.

Sam was bought up in an atmosphere where he never treated like a ten-year-old. Maybe he had forgotten what it was to be a kid after his mother's death. But after such a situation, Sam was forced to think about the past and all his scars turned to wounds again. He remembered how his mother had died and how painful it was. He really loved William as a friend and Sam was going through the same torture again! But finally, he asked for support. He had become a kid despite being on his own. He had returned to his childhood! Billy and Sam were so pure at that time that they almost forgot that they never spoke sweetly to each other and were practically hugging each other!

Jackson and Louis were on the way. Jackson was driving. They had no conversation. Both of them were lost in their own worlds. Jackson was missing his wife and was able to understand William's situation. He knew how bad it hurt. He also knew that there was no way out. He was also concerned about Catherine. He hoped she was fine. Louis was confused. When he thought of William, thoughts of Catherine disturbed him. When he thought of Catherine, thoughts of William disturbed him! Jackson and Louis were the responsible ones and had to handle the situation. They had emotions, but clearly understood that life wasn't always what it seemed to be, because it could shock and surprise one anytime and anyhow.

Unfortunately, Louis and Jackson were stuck in traffic. They didn't know what to do, Louis thought of calling Catherine's doctor. "Hello, Louis here, Catherine isn't well, I will explain everything later. Can you check on her at her hotel? We'll be there soon!"

The doctor was worried and said, "No worries, I'll go check!" Both of them kept their phones down and Jackson and Louis had no way out. There was too much traffic and Jackson exclaimed out of frustration "Damn it!" Things were messed up and they lost mental balance. They were frustrated, worried, confused and scared that things may turn worse.

The doctor reached Catherine's room by then with the hotel manager. They knocked on the door many times, but Catherine did not open the door. The hotel manager was forced to use the common card to open the door. They found Catherine lying on the rug. She looked like she was in a bad condition. The doctor and his team lifted Catherine and got into the ambulance. Just when they were leaving, Jackson and Louis reached. They were shocked and numb. They could only regret all that had happened. The situation explained everything and nobody was in a position to say anything. The doctor sat in the ambulance and Jackson and Louis sat back in the car and followed the ambulance. There was nothing to discuss, but they were in panic mode.

They soon reached the hospital and Catherine was admitted, and taken to the ICCU. Sam and Billy stood watching Catherine from outside. She was taken for treatment. Sam hugged Jackson tight, and burst out crying. Billy was embarrassed because the sour memories of when he misbehaved and abused William and did wrong to him were on his mind. He realized that it was, maybe, already too late.

They had no conversation! Absolute silence but the silence was killing them from within. They were desperately waiting for an answer. The media and press were in the lobby of the hospital although they weren't allowed to see William or any of his friends. They broadcasted the situation showing repetitive footage of the accident.

After a long externally patient and internally impatient wait, the doctor walked out of the ICCU. His head was down and the regret was clear on his face. Louis asked with hope in his voice, "How is aunty? Is she fine now?"

The doctor replied in a very low voice, "I'm extremely sorry. We failed saving Catherine. It was a major heart attack!" Sam and Louis collapsed and sat down on the couch.

Jackson was trying to be strong because he knew that it was time to manage the situation and not surrender before it. Billy was in tears, and was shocked. He said, with pain, "I never wanted this to happen!" Louis was torn apart and said, out loud, "How can God be so insensitive?"

They began crying. The doctor, because he treated Catherine for a very long time, knew that she was an angel in the human world. Sam was scared of losing his best friend, William, as well. They were so broken that they weren't even able to face each other!

Deep inside, in the water world, Nixie and the other mermaids were waiting for Yara to get back to life. They were desperate and happy. Nixie was congratulated, and each one told her, "You are a true friend!"

Another said, "We can't thank you enough!" Good wishes were said, over and over again, to Nixie, but she barely paid attention to any of them.

The mermaids noticed her weird behavior but thought she was probably worried for Yara and thus behaved this way.

Soon, Yara came back to life. She gradually opened her eyes. The moment she did, Nixie went close to her, crying. Nixie was happy, but had pain within. Yara stood up and all the mermaids came closer and hugged her. The place brightened up and celebrated another life of Yara's. This one, was what Nixie had given her. Yara hugged Nixie and they cried for a few minutes and were speechless. Nixie collapsed on the ground. The mermaids understood the matter but also knew the fact that they weren't in the position to help Nixie.

Nixie finally spoke to everyone. "I can't live without William anymore!" Her pain and feelings were strong. This was why high tides occurred. The weather had suddenly changed! It was getting darker and darker in the human world. The mermaids were not shocked, but were scared for the future!

Mermaids looked at Yara because she was the only mermaid who could control and explain to Nixie, and could influence her feelings. Yara knew that that it wasn't possible, but to respect the other mermaids' viewpoint, she did tried convincing Nixie on her wrong feelings. "I know, but this isn't in line with what is expected of the dignity of a mermaid. You can't love and live forever with a human!"

Nixie took some time and looked at Yara. Nixie looked at all the other mermaids. She was in love and there is no medicine for love! Nixie understood the dignity of a mermaid which was why she didn't wanted to be a mermaid anymore. But it wasn't in her control. Nixie yet found it important to talk about how she felt. She said, "I understand but I am in love and I don't know if it's right or wrong. I know that if William isn't a part of my life, my life won't make sense to me. I love you, Sakhi, and I did everything for you. You are my family! More than a friend! I also love William now, and isn't it my responsibility to make sure I don't hurt him and do everything for him, just as he did for me?" Yara was convinced, but she couldn't convince the others. Yara did not continue convincing anyone, which was why Lilly thought it was essential to convince Nixie and said, "But he is a human and humans have feelings that change! You can't trust him at all. He may forget about you in just a few days and he will move on!" Nixie found these words extremely offensive not to her but to her love!

Nixie wanted to convince everybody that she really loved him. "I broke his trust. He didn't! I lied to him. He didn't! I asked him to hate me but he still loves me and I can feel it. I left him midway but he wanted to continue. You say my love can be true but not his? That is impossible! I can feel his love. I see it in his eyes. If he wasn't in love with me truly, how did his tears cure Sakhi? Only love tears have that power. I needed him! Now, when he needs me, I shouldn't fail him!"

All the mermaids were convinced but worried, because they all knew that Nixie's wish would always remain a wish, it couldn't become a reality.

Nixie literally begged and said, "Please, help me! I did everything for everybody and now I can't even help myself, please do something, please!"

The mermaids realized that their love was no joke, but was extremely pure. They desperately wanted to do something. Nixie was so stressed that she wasn't able to think of a way out of all this. But she knew that if you want something done right, you have to do it yourself. This was not a mermaid teaching and it proved that she was feeling and thinking like a human.

This proved to be the reason for her suffocation in the water world. Yara wiped Nixie's tears. After Nixie calmed down, she was finally in a position to think. All mermaids could help, but they were prevented from promoting any mermaid towards taking up the wrong course of action, or doing something against their dignity.

Nixie finally came up with a fantastic solution. "We can ask for help from the King! He must have an answer and definitely, a solution!" Amanda wasn't convinced. She interrupted and said, "But the King wouldn't like to come across such feelings for a human!"

Nixie smiled after long and said, "Remember, the King mentioned that we work and accordingly get what we deserve. My work takes me in this direction. We can at least ask him once! There is no harm in it!" The mermaids looked at each other. They smiled and nodded, indicating an affirmation and soon, they formed a big round circle holding each other's hand.

Chapter 11

Love but Yet Distances!

Nixie and all the other mermaids were praying. After some time, the King appeared and all mermaids stood in rows. They had their head bowed down. Nixie was embarrassed. The King looked at Yara and said, "Your Sakhi turned the impossible to possible! You are very lucky!"

Yara smiled and said, "I truly am!"

Nixie was under pressure because she didn't know how to convince the King to grant her a solution. The King knew the reason for why he was called. He yet waited to hear from Nixie, but she was quiet and did not say a single word. The King then asked, "What else do you wish for?"

Nixie knew what she was asking for was very difficult to grant. But she believed in trying. She said, "King, I really love William. Please give me a solution so that I will be able to get back to him, please!" Nixie's tears were out of control. The King was serious but hid a smile that proved that he knew this was going to happen. He knew the future. He said, with no stress, "It's not possible!"

Nixie was broken, stranded and lost confidence. She said, "Please don't say so! I'll be broken! I can't live without him!"

The King wanted to test Nixie and said, "Nobody needs anybody for their survival. You are born an individual and will die an individual. How does survival relate with a human?"

Nixie never liked being argumentative. But she was aware that the King was testing her. She did not want to fail under any circumstance. She said, "When I was born, I was definitely an individual. I soon found reasons for survival and pursued happiness. But after being a human, my reason for survival and happiness was William. If he isn't a part of my life, I can never be happy!"

The King believed in Nixie's beliefs, but his test wasn't over yet. He asked again, "But if reasons change, they will change again. Life is a gift to living beings! Nobody has the right to create or destroy it. You must know that it's a crime! And maybe this was your destiny!"

Nixie was silent and had no answer. All the mermaids were worried for Nixie, especially Yara, because she was blaming herself for everything that had happened. Nixie regained her confidence and said, "It may be my destiny. But you said, that destiny can be changed to good or bad, through work and indeed our intensions. My work brought me to this point and my intention was always positive. I hurt somebody for self-centered reason and that's not fair, he loves me and I love him. We can at least be given a change! If my fate turns out to be strong, I'll accept it!"

Nixie, for the first time, had fire and confidence in her eyes, in such a complicated and tough situation where everybody seemed to be against her. Nixie had proved that nothing was impossible in any world, and that under any circumstances and one must never lose hope. The King was impressed and convinced. He was proud of Nixie, not because her intentions were always good, but because of the level of her determination and her honesty towards everything she did. Nixie had never complained in any situation and always believed in putting her best efforts to bring the worst situations under control.

The King smiled and said, "The both of you may have true love. But if you have really strong love, it can't break. You have to prove the power of your love! If the human accepts you as a mermaid after looking at you in your real form and does not die, or your power does not harm him in any aspect only then I will grant you a solution for it!"

It wasn't shocking for anybody that the solution could be tough. The shock was that the solution wasn't this - there was still a long way to win the battle! Nixie was not shocked, but was happy to know that there was a way out. She promptly said, "I agree!"

The King smiled and said, "Before you prepare to leave, have a look at what's going on earth! It is important for you"

Nixie was desperate and restless!

The King used magical powers and formed a big circle on the ground. All the mermaids gathered around the circle. The King threw some lights into the circle and in a few seconds, some pictures were seen in it. It was blurred in the beginning, but soon, it turned clear. It showed a live video of what was happening on earth in the lives of those that Nixie was concerned about.

The circle was more like a video playing. It showed the following scene.

William was in the hospital and the doctors were working hard for his life. William lay on the bed and the purification of his blood went on, William was doing poorly in health. The doctor also looked extremely stressed.

Nixie was deeply hurt and shocked. But that wasn't it. When Nixie saw what happened later, she was bruised and completely torn into pieces. She saw Jackson, Louis, Billy,

Sam and Catherine's doctor in the graveyard. They were all crying. The priest was praying for the dead to rest in peace. It was Catherine's burial! Catherine's body was inside the casket and was already placed under the ground. They buried her and the priest prayed for Catherine's soul. Later, one by one, Jackson, Louis, Billy, Sam and Catherine's doctor kept a circle of flowers each on the grave and prayed for Catherine. They were crying, but they knew they had to take care of William. They were also worried for William!

Nixie was emotionally handicapped. She looked at the King and he said, "You may leave, Nixie. But remember, this time, you won't be able to save William's life if the power of love between the both of you isn't strong!"

Nixie was lost for some time. She was not able to make a decision. If William died because of her, she wouldn't be able to forgive herself. She thought that if she stepped back, then she will regret it for the rest of her life, that she had a change of heart just out of fear of being responsible for something she quit! Nixie finally and firmly set her mind. She was mentally ready to leave. In reply to the King, Nixie said, "I'm ready!"

The King, all the other mermaids and Nixie travelled at great speed. They generated so much light, that the ocean seemed to be golden. The breeze blew faster, heavier and cooler. Trees began bending on the beachside. Underwater, at one point, everybody stopped. Nixie moved ahead. This time, she did not turn back. She was sure like never before, that the step that she had taken was correct. She believed in the power of the love between her and William. At the same time, William who was in hospital, began doing better. He was able to feel Nixie's presence.

William was trying to move and get off the bed like he wished to run somewhere. He finally said, something after a very long time. He said, "Nixie!" Then, he was back to unconsciousness. The doctor wasn't able to hear what he said, clearly. But, he did understood that he had said, a name. The doctor rushed out to William's friends, who were waiting for him. Fortunately, Billy was under the "friends" category. As soon as the doctor walked out, everybody stood up. The doctor said, "William just said, a name, it sounded like a girl's name! If you all can find that person and bring her here, it may help improve William's condition!" He went back immediately.

Everybody exchanged looks and Louis said, "It must be Nixie, but she proved to be such a cheater!" Jackson was convinced but wasn't able to accept that Nixie did all that. Sam felt the same way. Billy never bothered about Nixie and William's relationship. He had no judgments. But, he definitely thought that Nixie was a good girl! They were all extremely tensed!

Nixie finally reached the beach. This time, she came out of the water. Her hair and clothes dried in no time. She couldn't use magic in public so she hid herself in a corner and tried magically transporting herself. But each time she'd try, someone noticed her. Her magic failed every time. She finally decided to travel like humans do. She walked out of the beach and started looking for a taxi but maybe all this was her test, because none of the taxis stopped.

It was dark and Nixie had to walk a long way looking for a taxi. She finally realized that she could use magic to find a taxi. She used magic. In a second, she found a taxi. She sat in and told the taxi driver, "The nearest hospital!" she knew that William was admitted there. The streets were bright but

Nixie's world was dark. William meant the world to Nixie! The vehicles barely shifted because of the traffic jam. They were able to move only by a few inches at a time. It was nerve-wracking for Nixie and she used magic to clear her way to the hospital. The traffic started clearing in no time! The roads were suddenly easy to traverse and the taxi was comfortably speeding up!

Soon, in some time, Nixie had reached the hospital. She magically generated cash and paid the taxi driver. She ran into the hospital and stopped at the reception. She asked the receptionist where William Thomas was admitted.

She said "He is on the first floor". She was going to continue, but Nixie left before. Before Nixie left, she used magic and confused the receptionist so she couldn't stop her. Nixie used the elevator and reached the first floor. She was going to directly jump into the operation theater but Louis stopped her and they were all surprised to see her. She was embarrassed and had tears in her eyes. Louis hated her but the moment Nixie came, his hatred just vanished – as if it never existed.

Sam hugged Nixie tightly, and cried bitterly. Nixie ruffled his hair and hugged him and consoled him. Jackson and Billy were on top of the world. Louis asked, "Where have you been? You were in Finland. How come here?"

Nixie lied, saying, "I saw it in the news. I lied that I hated William, I really do love him, I am sorry!"

Jackson asked, "Then why did you lie?"

Nixie was confused and wanted to get into the operation theater. She said, "I can explain later, now I have to see William".

They all agreed. At the same time, the doctor walked out. He looked helpless. Nixie went into the operation theater. Before she entered, the doctor stopped her saying. "Hey, you can't get in!"

Before Nixie answered, Billy said, "She is Nixie. William needs her!" They were shocked to see Billy supporting Nixie.

Nixie said, "Please, doctor. It is important! I have to get in!" the doctor understood and let her in. He and William's friends waited outside. The moment Nixie went in, her speed of walking slowed down. She just looked at William. This was the first time ever when love was seen in Nixie's eyes. Maybe more, because she realized how important William was to her after she completely lost him once. This was the last and only chance for Nixie and William's love!

Nixie walked to William and sat beside him. She looked at him and closed her eyes. She generated magic in her palms and touched his head. Nixie opened her eyes and took her hand off. In just a few seconds, William woke up and saw Nixie. He thought he was dreaming, But Nixie said, "I'm sorry!" William did not believe it was Nixie standing in front of him. He wasn't grumpy at all and said, "Are you really here?" Nixie kept her hand on his face and said, "Yes, I'm really here!" William wanted to jump with excitement, but he began to cry. So did Nixie! William sat up straight and hugged each other.

Outside, William's friends and the doctor heard whispering. They thought that something was going on inside. They walked in and were surprised to see William awake. They thought it was magical! The doctor said, "Unbelievably magical!"

Nixie was crying bitterly and Louis said, "Thank you so much, God!" He hugged William and Sam hugged William and said, "Don't you ever go! Please!"

Sam looked at Nixie and said, "Both of you!" Then, Jackson hugged William and said, "Extremely happy to see you well!" Gradually, Billy walked closer with tears in his eyes. He had nothing to speak about. He was ashamed of his past behavior. William initiated and said, "Good to see you here!" Billy was guilty and said, "I'm sorry for everything I did wrong to you. Please forgive me!" William wanted to lighten the atmosphere and he was happy to see Nixie and said, "Oh come on!" William and Billy hugged each other! They were all very happy!

William then asked, "Where is mom? Why isn't she here?" Everybody looked at each other. They had no strength left to tell him about his mom, Nixie knew that his mom was no more in this world but she had to pretend like she didn't know! It was all very tough for Nixie but she had to do it.

Jackson walked closer to William and said, "We are really sorry!"

William casually said, "Sorry for what?"

Jackson was gathering his strength and said, "Unfortunately, Catherine had a heart attack after she heard of your accident, we couldn't save her!"

William was shocked and silent. He suddenly broke down loudly, and cried bitterly. They were all around to support him. But no words could console William. Nothing could bring back his mother! He said, out of extreme pain after being badly hurt, "Why did I get such life, why?"

Nixie knew that she was the reason why all that happened. Internally, it was killing her! Nixie was in a major dilemma. She wasn't able to make a decision on whether she should tell William or if she must just let go. She was responsible for that accident. But Nixie's life wasn't pleasant. She was going through the same and equal pain. But at the same time, Nixie knew that she had to talk to William.

The atmosphere was intense. William was completely broken. He recollected his past with his mom and cried harder! William felt like he was all alone in the world! Nothing was attracting him, but he thought of Nixie and told her, "Please don't leave me alone, ever, please!"

William seemed like a baby. He was crying for love. Nixie was under a lot of confusion! Nixie supported William and said, "Let anything happen. I will never ever leave you alone!" They shared a moment that included trust, respect and love towards for each other. William's only reason and interest of survival was Nixie. If Nixie would step back, it would have shaken William's world right from the roots, because he loved and trusted Nixie just like he loved and trusted his mom! William's and Nixie's love for each other was pure!

Nixie knew that it wasn't the right place and time to tell William anything about her, but Nixie didn't have much time. She had to ask William.

The doctor was checking William while everybody patiently waited. The doctor said, "You will all be happy to know that William is absolutely fine now and can get discharged! I'll go and check with the formalities."

Nixie and William were looking at each other and Jackson. Louis and Billy realized they must give them some space. Jackson said, to doctor, "Well, I'll come along." Louis and Billy said, together "Me too!" Sam was there.

Jackson dragged Sam out, saying, "You must be hungry. You surely must eat something!"

Sam innocently said, "I'm not hungry!" Jackson tried to make him understand. Finally, he dragged him out. They left. Nixie giggled. She made up her mind. William wasn't aware of what was going on in Nixie's head. William said, "I really love you Nixie!" Nixie smiled. She wasn't able to believe her destiny – the fact that she found somebody like William was still surprising.

She said, "I love you too!" After a pause, Nixie said, "William I want you to come to the beach with me, right now, please!"

William was shocked to hear that. At the same time, he realized that there must have been something important which was why Nixie asked. William said, "Okay! I will! Want me to ask the others?" William was trying to gauge whether Nixie wanted William alone to come, or if she wanted everybody else there. Nixie promptly responded saying, "Well, no. I just want you and me, nobody else. I know it's weird and awkward at the moment but I can assure you that it's really important, please trust me!"

William didn't know what Nixie was talking about. He still listened. He smiled and said, "You don't have to request me for anything and I do trust you!"

Nixie thought that it may take long to convince William in such a situation. She thought that William had lost trust in her. But Nixie was proved wrong. She was glad to be wrong. She found herself to be the luckiest on the planet and hugged William and said, "I thought you don't trust me anymore. Thank you for your trust! I really love you!" William had tears in his eyes but he wasn't upset anymore.

Louis walked in and happily said, "Well, William, would you like to walk? Or do you need a wheelchair?" This pretty much suggested that William was free to leave and was fit to walk.

William smiled and said, "Man I'm not that old and helpless yet! I want to walk a mile!" They were happy to see him so fit and fine! Initially, Nixie and Louis helped him get up. In the meantime, the doctor walked in and said, "I'll take you to the changing room!" William walked out with the doctor and Nixie and Louis walked down to the lobby. Nixie, Jackson, Sam, Louis and Billy were waiting for William. In some time, William came looking fresh. He looked very happy to have Nixie back with him, but he didn't show much of his happiness because he recently had lost his mother. He was trying to gather up his lost world! William wore loose pants and a loose t-shirt. The doctor came with him and said, "No tight outfits for at least another 15 days!" William nodded and the doctor said, looking at Jackson, "All formalities are done, you can leave now!"

The doctor then left and Sam said, "Now, no more crying! We're going back to the hotel and we will all have dinner together!"

Sam was excited and trying to lighten the atmosphere. Nixie looked at William. She was going to say something but William said before she could, "Guys, thank you for standing by me! You should all move to the hotel. I want to spend time on the beach with Nixie. Maybe we can talk for some time under nature's roof. You know how much we the love beach!"

William was lying because he didn't want anybody to doubt Nixie even for a single minute!" Respect for William grew in Nixie's heart. Jackson said, "Alright! You guys must have some time together. Don't worry about the media. We'll handle them!" Louis understood that they had to talk and said, "Yes, we'll see you both tomorrow then, take care!"

Sam was upset to hear that. But, he behaved maturely and said, "It's fine! We can have tomorrow's breakfast together!" They smiled. Billy spoke after a long time. "Well, you look great together!" Nixie and William said thanks. They were surprised to see Billy so genuine and understanding, but definitely appreciated the change in him.

Jackson then said, "Okay guys! We're leaving, both of you take care of yourself!" Everyone said goodbye to William and Nixie and waved their hands. After they left, Nixie and William walked out of the hospital. They looked around for a taxi. Nixie used magic to find one. They sat inside. William told the driver, "Take us to the beach!"

Nixie and William looked at each other. William could make out that Nixie was stressed about something. But, she didn't share it. They were both lost in thought! It was very complicated for William as he lost his mother and just been through so much trauma, he was only trying to handle himself!

Chapter 12

An Immortal Love that Began a New Journey

It was late at night. Nixie and William reached the beach. It was silent. Nobody was around and William and Nixie walked in. Nixie looked at the ocean without blinking. William felt the breeze. It was calming and romantic. Nixie was lost in memories and William was lost looking at Nixie. For a while, they did not talk because unspoken statements described everything.

Nixie turned towards William and said, "I don't know how you will react to this. But, this is my undisclosed reality!" Before William could question or could say anything, Nixie turned into a mermaid. William was thrilled. He was blown away and it was an extremely astonishing experience for him. The best part was that he didn't die. None of his organs were affected at all! Nixie's belief in her love and William's love for her proved right! Nixie wished for nothing else. No words were enough to explain their feelings. They understood each other's emotions well. William knelt down and touched Nixie's face, Nixie closed her eyes. It was the first time ever in history that a human had touched a mermaid!

William said, "I love your soul Nixie, no matter whether you are a human or a mermaid. Even if you were a witch, I'd love you exactly the way I love you now!"

Nixie was the happiest person on the planet. She found true love. She was proud of it. William felt like the luckiest man to find a soul like Nixie! Nixie then turned back to a human and got off the ground. Nixie and William smiled and hugged each other tight. They had calm eyes, satisfied minds, and stress-free brains.

Nixie then said, "William I want to tell you something."

William seemed curious and said, "Tell me!"

Nixie felt uncomfortable to tell him about the other task but she had to tell him the truth. She said, "William, in my world, the King takes all decisions and our future depends on his decision. I'm going to ask him for help now. I hope you understand."

William smiled and looked down at the ground. He looked back at Nixie and looked into her eyes and said, "Nixie if had to fight with world for you, trust me, I'd do it!"

William meant by what he said, they weren't just hollow words. William's feelings impressed Nixie. She thanked him.

Nixie joined her hands. Looking at her, William followed suit. Both closed their eyes and bowed their heads. Someone was coming close to them. They were unaware of who it was. The person initially seemed like a dot coming closer. Soon, they saw that he was a fit and muscular man about six feet tall in height. He was dressed like a priest, but seemed richer. He had a long silver beard and silver hair, a very clam face and a relaxed expression. Though he had wrinkles on his face, he was handsome. He came close and stood in front of Nixie and William. He was smiling and waiting for them to open their eyes.

Nixie felt the powerful man standing in front of her. She opened her eyes and exclaimed, "King!" The moment she spoke out, William also opened his eyes. They bowed their heads in respect for King. Nixie was overwhelmed, because she thought that finally, after many difficulties, they would be able to live together. Nixie hoped to hear from the King.

The King knew everything that was going on in Nixie's head. He said, "I am amazed. Tell me. What do you wish for?"

Nixie was desperate. She said, "King, we just wish to live together forever!"

They held each other's hands tight. The King looked at them. After a while, he said, "It's not possible to turn a mermaid into a human but I can turn a human to a merman. After turning into a merman, your memories from your human life will continue to exist and living with the past in a new world won't be possible. You can't live like a couple. You will be together but not as a couple!" It shocked Nixie and William. Nixie was going to leave William's hand and collapse, but William held her hand tighter and supported her. William understood Nixie's stress. This was why William said, on Nixie's behalf, "Please don't say so, please! I mean, there must be a way out!" The King gracefully said, "There is a way out but it is very difficult!"

Nixie stood straight and stopped crying, William and Nixie looked at each other and then Nixie said, "Please tell us!"

The King seemed happy. "If you want to live together, you will have to be reborn in the same world. This is the only way you can both live together! Do you agree?"

Nixie and William looked at each other and smiled. They looked at the King and said, together "Yes, we do!"

The King already knew their answer and said, "You have a day. Manage your life and when you're ready, come here. Your souls will leave for another life and your bodies will be dead!" Nixie and William looked at each other. When they turned to look at the King again, he had already left. The beach was empty. It was cold and absolutely silent!

Nixie and William held hands and walked out of the beach. They sat in the car and Nixie said, "William would you ever regret losing your life for me?"

William was happy but the trauma of the previous memories did pull his energy down. He wrapped Nixie tight in his arms and said, with confidence, "I was never so sure. I love you, Nixie. I will never ever regret this, trust me!" Nixie was relaxed. So was William. They looked happy, as if they were given a new lease of life! They knew that they were going to die, but they remained happy.

Time passed. Nixie and William lived for two days with everybody just like they lived and behaved before. They all had breakfast together. Everybody talked till late into the night. Jackson, Louis, Billy and Sam thought everything was okay. They cracked jokes to make William laugh and help him through this bad time. They also did the legal formalities following Catherine's death.

After two days, it was finally time to leave. They were checking out of the hotel. Sam was playing with a ball and they were waiting for their luggage, they were all just looking around. It was a very tragic journey for everybody.

Finally, when they were going to leave, Nixie whispered to William, "It's time!" they shared glances like they were preparing for something.

William loudly said, "Guys I want to tell you all something!"

Everybody looked at him and William said, "I was just wondering if you can take our luggage along to the airport. Actually, before we return, we both want to go to the beach once again!"

Jackson casually said, "But you guys will be late!"

William was trying to convince them and said, "Trust me, we'll be on time!" They looked at each other. Everyone was okay with it and therefore nodded.

Sam was a naughty boy and he teased William and Nixie, saying, "Ya, ya! We can understand your emotions!"

Everyone laughed. Nixie couldn't believe that she was meeting them for the last time! She had tears in her eyes. She was trying to hide her feelings. She knelt down before Sam and said, "You're an amazing kid! Take care!" She then hugged him. Nixie softly said bye. She stood up and said bye to everyone. They all said, bye, too. Sam thought it was a bit awkward, what Nixie had said, especially the way Nixie said, it. But he did not think much of it. After all, he was a kid! Nixie and William turned around and did not look back at anybody. They silently left while everybody was busy with the checking out formalities.

Nixie and William sat in the car. They weren't upset anymore. They had fiery eyes. They reached the beach. Each step they took had a feeling underfoot. They loved each other. They were confident and were all set for the journey ahead of them. They wanted to live life to the fullest extent. It seemed like words were desperate to come out, but smiles overlapped the words. They wanted to talk and just keep talking, but every time they'd look at each other, they'd just keep smiling.

William looked at Nixie before they entered the beach and said, "Nixie!" They stopped. Nixie turned to him and William asked, "Is it fine that we couldn't marry? Will you marry me in another life?"

Nixie blushed and said softly, "I'd be a fool if didn't. I will!"

William jumped off his feet with happiness. He lifted Nixie and turned her around. They were dancing like they were immortal! Suddenly, it began to rain.

William was surprised, and said, "It's raining! Unbelievable!"

Nixie smiled and said "It's raining because I am wishing for it to!" They danced and it rained heavily. The dark clouds covered the place like a shed. The clouds burst like never before and the breeze blew harder, faster and colder!

Nixie looked into William's eyes and asked, "Aren't you scared?"

William casually replied. "We are going to start a new journey together. We'll be together forever. Nothing can scare me! Why regret the past? Let's celebrate the future," they said dancing and celebrating a new journey. They were wet and their faces had turned pink because of the cold. They took off their shoes and sandals and danced like they were crazy. They weren't scared of anything. They were fearless! Nature celebrated with them. Butterflies were following Nixie's steps!

All the time, a question said to disturb Nixie. She finally decided to ask William. "William! Won't you miss your people here?"

William thought for a few seconds and smilingly said, "I already lost my family and my friends will surely understand me. Nixie, I love you! I can do anything for you!"

Nixie was happy, but numb. They then held hands and walked in the ocean. They walked slowly, feeling each step, just looking at each other. No one else in the world would be this happy to know he was dying. Water covered half of their bodies and they weren't afraid at all!

Nixie said sweetly and hopefully, "We'll meet again in another life!" and William added, "And then we'll never separate!"

Nixie smiled and said, with determination, "Never ever!" They hugged each other. Their hair flew in the breeze. They hugged each other so tight as though they would never let go. They had no concern with what was going on around them! They peacefully closed their eyes and in just a second, their spirits left their bodies. Their bodies fell. Their spirits were seen up high on the sky, looking way more beautiful than anything else. It looked like a golden light beam.

They were extremely happy. Nixie's spirit looked like a mermaid and William's was like a human. Soon, their spirits disappeared. Lots of butterflies gathered around them. It was unusual because butterflies are never seen near the dead. But there, butterflies gathered like they were in a beautiful garden. Nixie's dead body turned into a mermaid's body because she was originally a mermaid. The King appeared in the sky and used magic. The butterflies roamed around Nixie's body and it turned into a human form. The King then disappeared and so did the butterflies.

The strangest part was that Nixie and William's bodies were smiling. Soon, they turned neutral. In just a few minutes, a group of young adults walked on the beach. They wore shots and were preparing to play volleyball! Their ball slipped from Neil's hand. One of the boys in the group went to fetch the ball. They came to Nixie's and William's dead bodies. He noticed the bodies.

He got scared and yelled, "Aaaah! Oh my God! Guys come on! Come here, fast!"

All his friends gathered around the dead body and didn't know what to do. They were frightened but they knew that they had to do to do the right thing.

They looked at each other. Rim pulled out her phone out of the pocket of her shorts and called the cops. She said, "Hello, this is Rim here. We need somebody here on the beach. Two dead bodies are lying on the shore!" After a while, she kept the phone down. They sat some distance away and didn't want to be a part of any sort of trouble.

Rim was annoyed and said, "What the hell! We were here for fun and this is what happens!"

Neil was less annoyed, but more worried and said, "Forget about the fun! I hope the cops don't investigate us. I mean, my parents will kill me!" Robin, Amie and Zac were so scared that they didn't even utter a single word. They had poker faces!

Rim was concerned about the fun. He looked at Robin, Amie and Zac and said, aloud, "Guys, don't be so childish! You guys are acting as if someone is dead!" Robin was irritated and grumpily said, "Someone is dead, you fool!"

Rim found it offensive. He said, "Did you kill them? If you didn't, why are you so worried about it? Fool!" They were bugged, but it was useless to explain to them. They said arguing. By then, the cops had arrived. They first cordoned off the area. When the group of young adults tried to say something, they were asked to shut up. "No conversation! Just facial expressions!" The cops found the details from William's pocket and called Jackson from William's contact.

The flight departed from the runaway. Nixie, William, Jackson, Sam, Louis and Billy were supposed to be on the flight, but they were all on the beach. Jackson, Sam, Louis and Billy couldn't believe what was happening and Sam was crying bitterly. It was a great disaster for everybody. Sam held Jackson and yelled, "Why dad, why?" Jackson was speechless and Louis was shocked. He was expressionless, and had tears flowing from his eyes. Billy was also in tears!

The group of young adults spoke to the cops and left.

Soon, the ambulance and media arrived. William and Nixie's bodies were kept in the ambulance. Their friends were in tears. It had turned out to become a funeral on the beach. William and Nixie's spirits was seen in the sky. They saw everything happen before them - Nixie did magic and a lot of butterflies fluttered around their friends. Nixie and William looked happy and didn't want their friends to be broken after their death, Nixie had used magic to give them strength to always stay strong! Their friends were able to feel Nixie and William's presence but couldn't see them. Soon, their spirits vanished.

James' diary was still lying on the island.

Nixie and William's love was alive, although they were dead.